NOT QUITE DEMONS

Angel Bay Mysteries Book 2

MELANIE JAMES

SUMMARY

With one major mystery solved, Emmy and her friends planned to finally concentrate on something a little more enjoyable—hot guys. But their hopes are dashed when the dramatic arrival of a mysterious stranger heralds the beginning of yet another whodunnit.

Extortion, murder, kidnappings. It seems like Angel Bay is going to Hell in a handbasket. With so many people keeping secrets, just about everyone becomes a suspect. Emmy knows it just might take collaboration with the dark side to get to the bottom of things—in more ways than one!

EDITION LICENSE NOTES

Not Quite Demons
1st Edition
By Melanie James
Copyright © 2021 by Melanie James
Editing: Black Paw Edits
Proofreading: AVCProofreading
Proofreading: Book Nook Nuts
Formatting: Black Paw Formatting

ACKNOWLEDGMENTS

Ron – Thank you for keeping me sane. I love you always.
Julia – You are my girl and I love you. I can't possibly thank
you enough!

To my readers. Thank you for sticking with me. Without you, none of this would be possible.

CHAPTER ONE

The oversized wicker chair on the front porch of our gift shop created the perfect morning perch. Closing my eyes, I filled my lungs with the crisp air fresh off the shimmering blue waters of Angel Bay.

"Heaven on Earth," I whispered into my cup of tea.

"Good morning, Harry," I greeted my companion. I doubt the cool air was a treat for him—even with the tiny blue sweater Chloe had knitted for him.

Just to clarify, Harry is a bearded dragon who had been abandoned when Midge, the previous owner of our store disappeared, and her belongings washed up on Angel Beach. We found him in the store when Heaven sent us here on assignment.

He's a friendly little guy and a good listener when I need to take stock of my life—out loud and without judgment. I'm sure you know what I mean.

"This is my Heaven all right, Harry. I don't think it's too far off to describe our new home like that, at least in some ways. After all, I believe I have a qualified opinion on the matter."

Harry blinked, nonchalantly.

"Of all places, why was I sent here you ask?" Sipping my tea, I scanned the sunny bay and idyllic waterside town of Angel Bay.

"That's a very good question. As you probably guessed, I wasn't sent here alone. Chloe and Jade, my partners and my best friends, came along for the assignment. And I think it's because we all have one thing in common, we're misfits."

Harry raised his little hand, seemingly to ask another question.

"Yep, I'm sure. We're all misfits. We were told we'd never be real angels because we were each conceived and born in Heaven. And according to the matriarchy, that's cheating the system. Apparently. Blah, blah, blah. But back to my sisters. Well, not biologically speaking we aren't. But we're so close, the three of us like to think of ourselves as sisters."

Harry bobbed his head from side to side. I'd read, in one of our books on bearded dragon research, it was a common gesture for the little critters.

"Anyway, Heaven stepped in and gave us a mission: to fulfill our destiny and become full-fledged angels by performing angelic work for the benefit of the mortal citizens of Angel Bay, to bring peace and justice to the community, and to live up to the high moral standards expected from angels."

While Harry didn't exactly laugh—because I don't know if bearded dragons can laugh—his mouth dropped open as if he thought it was pretty damn funny that high moral standards were our goal.

"Seriously. Yeah, moral standards. And we've been trying. The problem is, we've been more or less dumped here with vague instructions and zero help from above." I jabbed my index finger toward the sky.

"In fact, we've realized this is a do-it-yourself mission. We can't even call home for advice." Defiantly tilting my face toward the heavens, I raised my voice.

"Even if we consider that we might have been abandoned, we've vowed to prove our angelic worth."

I heard Harry sigh. Seriously.

"We're practically angels, but we're also young women who have been thrown into the confusing and temptation filled mortal world. There's work, and paying bills, feeling like crud, and trying to decide what to eat. Or what to wear. Sure, we had a short crash course in Mortal Living 101 with Mrs. Portobello, but nothing she could have taught would have ever prepared the three of us for the mortal plane. We were the only heavenly beings, up to this point, to never step foot in the human world. We weren't born on Earth. We didn't die and pass on to Heaven. We were born in Heaven. There wasn't a single thing about our upbringing in Heaven that could have prepared us for living on Earth. Then there was the even shorter time with Natasha, our program director. The only thing we ever learned from her was that we didn't make the Heavenly portals blink red or green when we passed through, making us the only beings who were completely undetectable."

I sighed, quite dramatically. It felt good to expel my thoughts, even if I was expelling said thoughts to a bearded dragon.

"Is that all I'm worried about, you ask? Not even close! I haven't even touched on relationships—friendly or otherwise. Which brings up the big wide world of boys, and all the different and frightening ways our bodies react to them. Things we know nothing about and could never have prepared for. You know, boys, love, sex."

The more I thought about our predicament and talked it out, the more thoughts filled my mind.

"What about your parents? They had a loving relationship," I said in my best bearded dragon voice. Funny thing, even when I spoke as Harry, I gave him the same silly British accent Chloe did.

"You're right, Harry. My parents did have a wonderful marriage filled with love, but I don't know how they reached that point in their relationship. I've never witnessed the mechanics of watching someone fall in love or lust. Our only guide in these earthly matters has been our well-read collection of paranormal romance books, the complete series of Dark Beasts."

"Beeeaaaassstssss," he whispered.

"Oh yeah, and it's come in handy. I'm not talking about the sometimes vague and often weird metaphors for sex the writers use in the books. What I'm talking about is learning how to understand the beasts. The male variety."

"Tell me." I could swear the lizard whispered.

"So, there's this guy I met. He's around my age, in his early twenties. A sexy, hot biker by the name of Zane. The attraction I feel for him is off the charts. He's kind. He's smart, super good looking, and extremely confident. For a young man, he seems so...wise. Like he's really into ancient philosophers, and not in a boring way, quite the opposite. But there is something dark about him, along with a certain swagger. He's oozing erotic energy. His kiss makes me feel like such a naughty angel."

I remembered everything about the way Zane's kiss made me feel.

"And that turns me on."

"Yessss," he whispered.

I eyed Harry suspiciously, shrugged and decided to keep on going. Life was already strange. At this point, would it really make a difference if our bearded dragon actually had the ability to speak?

"Of course, it has to be complicated. His mother, Eve, happens to be Angel Bay's resident witch. His father is some rich playboy devil, who I have yet to meet. And I mean like the real deal kind of devil. I don't know if he has horns and such...and oh yeah, there's the local motorcycle gang, the Hellions. They are a colony of wild demons who Eve conjured up from Hell. But Zane has me so fricking hot, I don't even care. It's crazy, I know. But his kisses, and the way he touches me. I can barely control myself. And in my dreams, I certainly let myself go wild. But what's crazier, imagining I'm having a conversation with a reptile, or that I've decided I'm ready to give in to my carnal desires for Zane? I'm serious. Next chance I get, I'm going to go for it. All the way."

"Such a filthy ho," Harry growled.

"What? How——" I nearly shouted, spinning to face the little dragon.

Lo and behold, it was Chloe voicing the part of Harry all along. She'd been lurking nearby the whole time. At some point, the little smart-ass had crept up to the table and picked up Harry.

"That was a very interesting summary. My favorite part was how you see me and Jade as your best friends and sisters."

"You really shouldn't sneak up on people. I might have to take back everything nice I said."

"I know Harry is a good listener and all, but next time you want to sort out whether you're going to act on your depraved desires, just come and talk to me or Jade."

"The two of you are the worst influencers in my life!" I teased. I just couldn't help it. She was making it too easy.

She rolled her eyes and continued like I hadn't even said a word. Figures...

"By the way, you left out something important that we still need to look into—those wilderness areas Eve and her demon bikers were so determined to save from the developers. Doesn't it make you curious? I mean, what's their interest in the land?"

"I assumed they didn't want more people moving into the area who might discover their secret. I guess, I haven't given it much more thought."

"Maybe. But they might have their own malicious intent. They could be making moonshine... or maybe they've set up a secret drug lab in the woods. Who knows?"

"We can't always think the worst of people, Chloe. Not even if those people are witches and demons." I tried to reassure Chloe—and even myself, if I was being completely honest.

"Maybe it makes me a lousy angel, but I trust those Hellions about as far as I can throw them and that's not very far. Doesn't it bother you that Zane hangs out with them a lot? He's practically a member of their biker gang, just saying."

Chloe's question was a familiar subject. I'd asked myself the same question dozens of times, but managed to knock it back down like I was playing mental whack-a-mole. I tried not to look too hard at his personal friendship with the Hellions because I worried I'd find a fatal flaw in Zane.

Still, Chloe and I shared a certain personality trait, not curiosity exactly, but something more which drove us to investigate everything. As for me, it was because I needed to know the world around me was good and just. And to fix the things which weren't.

I had to change the subject.

"Do you know if Jade had any luck trying to call Mrs. Portobello or Natasha?" I asked, hoping we'd finally made contact with our Angel Academy instructors.

"Nope. Nothing. Just like always," Chloe sighed.

Her answer was really no surprise. We'd repeatedly tried to call and text our connections in Heaven, the polite and humble Miss Portobello and the ominous and intimidating Natasha. Other than receiving a single text message advising us to help the good people of Angel Bay, we were, so far, unsuccessful in trying to communicate with them.

Jade stormed onto the front porch, carrying a small radio that squealed with the most annoying noise known to human or angel. "Batten down the hatches, ladies. We've got a severe thunderstorm warning with possible tornadoes heading our way."

"Are you sure the storm is going to hit Angel Bay?" I asked, completely surprised by the development.

"Yep. Check out those dark clouds. Something's brewing across the bay, and quickly." She pointed toward the clouds, which had already grown into an ominous dark mass. "Look how choppy the water is now."

The gentle waves I'd found beautiful not so long ago, now thrashed over the sandy beach. Large whitecaps curled in the distance, driven by an unexpected gusty breeze.

Jade and I battled gale force winds which were suddenly upon us to take down the "Open, Come On In!" flags.

Chloe hurriedly wrapped Harry in her arms. She rushed him inside, securing him safely in his habitat.

Gathered behind the safety of the service counter, we watched the dark clouds rapidly approach. A continuous drumroll of thunder rolled over the open water, thrilling us. You have to understand, there are no storms in Heaven. Consequently, we were awed by the beautiful yet frightening dark power of nature.

"Look at that lightning. It's awesome and scary at the same time." Chloe summed up our feelings.

Within minutes, the dark clouds unleashed a torrential

downpour. We gasped, having never witnessed such a display. It was like nothing we could have ever imagined.

Day had become night. The lights flickered in our store before everything suddenly went dark.

Jade futilely slapped at the light switches, trying to force the power to come back on. White and blue flashes from the nearby lightning invaded the darkened store, followed by several loud cracks of thunder that shook our building and everything in it.

"Jesus Christmas! This isn't cool anymore!" Chloe squeaked.

Jade was focused on striking a match. "Ta da!" she yelled, announcing the successful lighting of a lantern. "I knew this kerosene lantern would come in handy one day."

Grabbing another pack of matches, I went to work lighting several candles until a cozy yellow glow enveloped the store. "There—" I was just about to compliment my own work when I spun around and saw him. Paralyzed by the surprise encounter, I greeted the stranger with a silent, stupefied stare.

He was well built and seemed tall, easily over six feet. The stranger was well-dressed in a black three-piece suit with a white button-down shirt and a blood red tie. He was undeniably handsome with his high cheekbones and rugged jaw. His impeccably styled jet-black hair added to his allure. He looked as if he was perhaps in his forties, yet younger at the same time. And somehow, he was perfectly dry. Astonishingly, not a drop of rain had hit him.

"Strange," I mumbled.

"Sorry to have surprised you." He spoke with an accent which I assumed was British. "I'm Ash," he said, extending his hand.

"Emmy," I replied with a limp handshake.

"Is Emmy short for something? Ash asked.

"Uhh, Emerald," I stammered.

"What a beautiful name."

"I—I didn't realize we had any customers."

"Of course. I'm sorry. Allow me to explain. I happened to dodge in here just before the rain came crashing down." He smiled at me.

I wasn't sure if I amused him or if he was just being pleasant. It seemed like his eyes pierced deep inside of me, as if he were searching for something. What he searched for, I had no idea.

I finally released my hand from his strong grip. "Feel free to look around, Mr. Ash. The power's out, but we have plenty of candles."

"Ash. Please just call me Ash. And I have been perusing your excellent selection of antique books. It's very impressive."

"Thanks. Most of the inventory was already on the shelves when we took ownership. We still haven't inventoried all of them."

"I was pleasantly surprised at this old edition of The Lesser Key of Solomon. I'd like to purchase it," he said, handing me a tattered leather-bound book.

Unfamiliar with the title, I handed it back. "Name your price and it's yours."

Chloe and Jade wobbled closer like a pair of low-budget robots. It was painfully obvious they were completely spellbound by the mysterious and handsome stranger.

My entranced friends gently bumped into me, forcing an introduction.

"These are my business partners and friends, Jade and Chloe."

Giving them each a light handshake, he replied, "Call me Ash. It's nice to meet you. Such lovely young ladies. I believe I've found my new favorite shop."

Removing a folded wad of hundred-dollar bills from his coat pocket, he handed it to me. "I trust this is a fair payment for the book. Good day, ladies," he said, and left as quietly as he had arrived.

As soon as Ash left, the rain stopped, and the dark clouds disappeared. The power in the store flickered back to life.

"That was weird." Jade crossed her arms over her chest and snuggled into herself like she was trying to shake off a sudden chill.

I shrugged and counted the money before placing it in the register. Weird was a relative term these days. "He gave us five thousand dollars for that old moldy book," I said, completely shocked.

"Oh my God! We just met a real honest-to-goodness sexy ass vampire!" Chloe yelped.

I must have looked at her like she'd grown a pair of horns. "What in the world are you talking about?"

"Oh, come on, Emmy. You had to notice—the sudden storm, the dark clouds, the power outage, the super-hot mysterious guy with an accent who suddenly appeared in our store? He was just like the vampire from Dark Beasts, book nineteen."

"The Boy Necks Door?" I asked.

"No, the other vampire book."

"It Stakes One to Know One?"

"That's the one!"

Jade clucked her tongue off the roof of her mouth. "He was hot, for sure. And here I was thinking maybe he was a movie star, or perhaps a salesman peddling timeshares. But a vampire? Of course. It's so obvious. I don't know why I didn't think of it." She shrugged, mocking Chloe.

"I'm ninety-nine percent sure he wasn't a vampire. I'm more interested in why he paid so much for that old book. It was practically falling apart. I probably would've given it to him for free," I said, trying to remember the title of it.

"I, for one, will be keeping an eye out for the mysterious Mr. Ash. And when I show you the undeniable proof that he's a vampire, I just might accept your apologies—no guarantees." Chloe huffed.

CHAPTER TWO

*F*our peaceful weeks passed by since the well-dressed stranger had visited our store. That's not to say things weren't uneventful, at least on the romance front. The enigmatic force which drew Zane and I together was stronger than ever. We saw each other every single day. Sometimes just for lunch, other days for an evening walk, and other times an evening out together. But not a day went by without one of his sweet kisses and his erotic touch.

I knew as sure as I knew the sun would come up in the morning, if left unchecked, things between us were heading to a new level. I felt like one of those surfers carefully balancing themselves to enjoy the thrilling speed from the undisputable power of a massive wave. Eventually, the wave would break on the shore, crashing down on the surfers who decided to ride it out to the end.

So, that was me. The virgin surfer trying to decide when, or if, I should break free before the undeniable forces of nature crashed over me. To be honest, I was more thrilled than afraid.

But in Angel Bay, things are never as peaceful as they may

appear. And a distracting mystery was just what I needed to get my mind off things.

"Good morning, Mary," I said, welcoming our next-door neighbor, Mary O'Brien. "You're our first customer of the day. Can I help you find anything? Chloe put together some nice little baskets filled with a variety of herbal teas. They make great gifts."

"Oh, no thanks. I just stopped by for...for a little advice." She glanced skittishly around the room.

It seemed strange for my forty-year-old neighbor to come to me, a twenty-two-year-old amateur for advice.

"Okay, but full disclosure—I'm sadly inexperienced in just about everything from business to romance."

"Us too," Chloe said.

Jade and Chloe's surprise arrival caught me off guard. And leave it to Jade to be brutally honest.

"Jeez, Mary. You look rough, like you're barely holding it together. Are you okay?"

"I don't mind telling you girls, I'm falling apart like a hooker's panties on payday."

"Yeah, we've been practicing white magi—" Chloe said before I cut her off.

"We've helped quite a few people. What's troubling you?" I asked.

"Perhaps 'advice' wasn't the right word to describe what I need. I should say I'm looking for some assistance. Gossip around town is that you girls have a special, if not a rather unconventional, skill set which you've used to solve a variety of problems."

Mary was unusually fidgety.

"Go on," I prodded her.

"First, this must be strictly confidential."

"Of course. Completely," I said.

"Good. I'm glad I can trust you." She dug around in her

purse. Retrieving her cellphone, she unlocked the screen and took a deep breath before handing it to me.

"These pictures were emailed to me. I don't know who sent them, but it was someone using a fake identity."

I had to blink three times before I understood who the nearly naked woman was. "Mary! These are pictures of you!"

Each image showed Mary scantily dressed or nude, in one seductive pose after another.

"Who? What? Why?" The words flew from my mouth.

"I'm being blackmailed. Whoever sent these pictures is demanding I transfer nine thousand dollars to his account within ten days or he is going to send them to Tim, and tell him I've been having an affair, or worse."

"So, Tim wasn't behind the camera? Did your secret lover take the pictures or was it someone else?" Chloe asked, trying to comprehend the situation.

"No! I mean, yes, someone other than Tim took these, but I don't know who. I have no memory of posing like this, and trust me, I'd remember. It's like I have this big, dark, empty place in my mind when I try to remember when these pictures were taken. I just don't understand it."

"The easiest explanation would be that the pictures are fakes. There are a lot of people who are quite good at creating bogus photos with their computers," I suggested.

"I thought maybe that was the case, but then I noticed this." She tapped the screen until it zoomed in on a small dark spot on her inner thigh.

"See that? It's a bruise. I got that bruise last month when I bumped into a sharp corner on my deck. Nobody but Tim knew it was there. And this mole here. How could anyone fake that? They'd have to know some very intimate details about my body. These are legitimate pictures. And it's scary to think that there's someone out there—other than my husband, who took photos of me like this."

"Have you talked to the police about this?" I asked.

"Absolutely not. You think that Officer Daryl would believe me? Do you think he's going to believe that I was suddenly struck with a case of selective amnesia? The first person he'd question about the case would be Tim, and that's the last thing I want to happen."

"It's just that I don't know if we can help you with this, Mary."

"Maybe you can. If you can find a way to restore any lost memories, maybe I'll learn how this happened and who's behind it. It's one thing to be blackmailed, but to have your brain toyed with...well, it's a whole new level of crazy."

"I can only promise we'll look into it. Who knows? Maybe there is a way to restore lost memories. We'll let you know," I said.

"That was an unexpected and bizarre start to the day," Jade said after Mary had left the store.

"Dang it," Chloe mumbled.

"What is it?" I asked.

"I was wondering about how someone could just lose their memory of having all those nude photos done, and I think I know how."

"What do you mean?"

"I mean, whoever took those pictures is trying awfully hard to stay anonymous, which I guess is expected, but I think he made her forget. Somehow. Then I got to thinking..."

"Oh, here we go," Jade groaned.

"Seriously! I got to thinking about how vampires have the ability to control their victims and then, poof! They wipe out any memories of what happened. It really is the perfect crime! I should've checked Mary for bite marks."

"There's a problem with your theory, Sherlock," I said.

"Why would a vampire with mind control powers need to

blackmail Mary? If he needed money, couldn't he just stop by the bank and charm the teller into handing him a whole bag full of cash?"

Chloe folded her arms over her chest and rolled her eyes. "The bank closes at five. It's still daylight then. Everyone knows vampires are allergic to sunlight. Duh."

"She has a point," Jade said.

"Really, Jade? You're going to play along and humor her and that wild vampire theory? If we're going to look into this, we have to be clear-eyed and levelheaded. We should use logic and reason."

"Since when is clear-eyed and levelheaded our style? And logic? Reason? Those are just fancy words for guesses," Jade replied, her wry smile told me she was genuinely enjoying my growing frustration. "Sometimes, a good dose of senseless lunacy is helpful, if not entertaining."

"Exactly!" Chloe yelped. "And if there is one thing I know about, it's senseless lunacy."

"Here's my suggestion. Chloe, you and Jade look through the books, see if you can find a way to restore missing memories. I'm going to ask around and see if anyone has seen the mysterious Ash. I seriously doubt he's a vampire, but I agree we should consider him a possible suspect. Maybe if we rule him out, we can drop your crazy vampire theory."

"By asking around, you mean you're going to meet up with Zane. Isn't it kind of hard to talk to him with your tongues stuck in each other's mouths," Jade scoffed.

"Oh, I'm sure we'll take a few minutes to talk first." I gave her a playful shove.

Later that morning, I decided to go for a walk. I needed some space and time alone to ponder Mary's predicament—without Chloe's supernatural theories or Jade's mischievous ribbing. Five minutes later, my mind was buzzing as I tried to gain another perspective.

What if Mary wasn't telling us the whole story? Was she actually involved with someone else and got caught up in a blackmail scheme? It's hard to imagine anyone posing for those kinds of pictures without being intimately involved with someone.

Once I started down the rabbit hole, my thoughts began to spiral out of control.

Unless...unless she ended things with her paramour, and he took it badly. He could have resorted to blackmail. Or he could be threatening her purely for revenge. And the amnesia? I just don't get it. Why would she make it up? Is she hoping we will somehow provide the alibi she needs to convince everyone she was brainwashed or something equally bizarre? I have no idea how that would even work.

I hate thinking the worst about people. It goes against everything in my nature. It's so dark and contrary to how I've always looked at the world. No matter how hard I had tried to entertain Chloe's vampire theory, I just couldn't bring myself to believe there was a supernatural reason behind Mary's ordeal.

By the time I'd made my way around the second corner, I'd only managed to complicate the issue with more questions than I started with, and most disappointingly, added the aura of suspicion to Mary.

No wonder Chloe preferred to suspect a blackmailing vampire as the bad guy. It kept the human citizenry of Angel Bay in a more favorable opinion.

But then, I remembered Daryl's bout this summer with memory loss.

One night he was hellbent on searching for the truth about Midge's disappearance, and the next day, he didn't remember bringing it up and considered the case closed. That has never been satisfactorily explained to me. It must be a separate issue, though. I better not mention it to Chloe, or it'll muddy everything up with more wild assumptions. One case at a time.

My sweet tooth must have been in charge of navigation

that morning. I found myself stopping to briefly admire the beautiful blooms of a lush flower garden gracing the front yard of Kathy's Cafe. She had certainly spent considerable time and effort creating such a welcoming space. The delicious bakery scents directed me to make a hard left turn, and drew me right through the door.

"Good morning, Kathy."

Like Mary, Kathy was another of Angel Bay's successful small business owners. At nearly forty years old, she seemed experienced, cheerful, and happily married. I came to look at her as another positive role model.

"What can I get you?" Kathy asked. No "Good morning, Emmy" or "How are you doing?" Her voice seemed flat, lacking her usual sunny inflection.

Strange. Is she avoiding eye contact with me?

"Let's see," I said, bending down to check out the selection.

"Two chocolate frosted cream filled Long Johns with rainbow sprinkles for Chloe. They are her favorite. Jade likes the cinnamon twist tiger tails, so two of those please. And I'll have one of those jumbo glazed cinnamon rolls."

Kathy quietly placed my order in a pastry box and rang up the total on the cash register.

"I'm sorry, Kathy. But I am going to intrude. Are you feeling okay? You seem so blue. Something must be wrong. Is there anything I can do to help?"

"Uh...Emmy." Kathy exhaled like someone just deflated her. "Something awful is happening to me. I—I'm embarrassed, ashamed, and I have no idea how it happened."

She picked up her phone, hesitating to show it to me. "It's all foggy like—"

She was sounding and acting a heck of a lot like Mary.

"Like you have amnesia? About how someone was able to get compromising photos of you for blackmail?"

"Yes! How did you know?"

"Because you're not alone. Someone else in town came to us with the same predicament this morning."

I actually felt slightly relieved to hear Kathy's bad news. It meant Mary was telling the truth. And so was Kathy. With any doubts I had in Angel Bay's character erased, I resolved myself to get to the bottom of things.

"Don't you worry about it, Kathy. Chloe, Jade, and I are on this. We'll find out who did this and how. And we'll keep it secret."

"You'd do that for me?"

"Of course, us girls have to stick together. I'll get in touch with you soon," I said, paying for the treats.

She closed the register and waved off the cash I slid over the counter.

"No charge," she said, looking slightly relieved. Probably because she knew she wasn't the only one facing a terrifying blackmail scheme.

I had one hand on the door when I decided to spring a question on her. "Say, Kathy, have you had a customer named Ash recently, like within the last month? He's tall, handsome, dark haired, very movie-starrish."

"This time of year, I get a lot of vacationing customers, so I can't say for sure who I've met. But offhand, nobody like that stands out."

"Thanks, Kathy. Just curious."

On my way home, I reexamined the situation.

Are there more victims than just Kathy and Mary? Maybe this has been going on for a long time? Who knows? Maybe there are dozens of victims. Multiple cases with the same weird amnesia...what logical explanation can there be?

A chilling thought rippled through me.

Maybe Chloe is on the right track. Those women just might be the victims of a villain with a supernatural power. She doesn't seem to have met Ash, but then again...

"Breakfast!" I announced, setting the donuts on the counter.

Jade and Chloe emerged from the back room. Jade carried an oversized ancient book, which I assumed was one of our many volumes of angelic cures. Chloe carried a notebook and several paperback volumes of the Dark Beast series.

"As you can see, we're already on the case," Chloe said.

It was apparent she was quite serious about her vampire theory.

"Cases," I replied.

"When I stopped at the bakery, Kathy told me that she also fell victim to the same blackmail and amnesia scheme as Mary. I suspect there are more cases out there."

"Or there soon will be, unless we figure out who's behind this," Jade said.

Swapping their books for pastries, they joined me at the counter. Chloe opened her notebook, and between bites of her donut, she explained what she'd been working on.

"I'm getting the vampire M.O. down. You have to understand that all of the vampire's qualities and abilities have been specifically developed to make him—or her—the perfect predator. I've written each down, and after I read them off, I want you guys to vote yes or no as to whether the mysterious Ash meets these specifications."

"Okay, but you are already assuming he is behind all the extortion," I replied.

"Let's just play along," Jade said. "Go ahead, Chloe."

"Vampires don't hunt like tigers. They are passive, like carnivorous plants, you know Venus fly traps. In the book, *Stakes One to Know One,* the vampire has the following gifts: extremely attractive, meticulously groomed hair, a sexy foreign accent, well dressed, impeccable manners."

"Sure. I'll say yes to those," I said.

"Ditto," Jade replied. "But I bet a lot of people could fit that bill without being vampires. What really IDs him?"

"I'm glad you asked. You see, the vampire is the ultimate honey-trap. They have all those qualities to draw in their victims, to put them at ease, to ultimately seduce them. Here's the more specialized abilities that help vampires take down their victims: mind-reading, mind-control, mind-blowing sexual talents, and an insatiable lust for human blood."

"Man, I really hate guys who love to play head games," Jade groaned.

"How in the world would we know if Ash had any of those things?" I asked, ignoring Jade's little joke. "He was attractive and all but come on. Three young women all alone in a store? We would've looked like an all-you-can-eat buffet to a vampire. Wouldn't he have sucked up our blood?"

Chloe said, waving her arms as if she could physically ward off our doubt, "Yes, he would've. After an all-out orgy. And we'd never remember it. It's what they do."

"I promise you, Chloe. No orgies or bloodletting occurred that day," I said.

Jade examined Chloe's neck. "We'd at least have bite marks to show for it."

"Hold on one second," I said, pinning Chloe against the counter and checking the other side of her neck. "Are these... oh my God! Look at this, Jade!"

"What? What! What is it?" she yelped. "Fang holes? What?"

"Hmm. Is this how vampires mark their orgy victims?" Jade whispered, trying to sound concerned for Chloe's life.

"Yep. Right after they slip them a psychic roofie," I said.

Chloe's little body trembled, and she made a whimpering sound. "Oh, Jesus. My mind's been wiped clean, I bet. We ought to get to a clinic and get tested for STDs. Who knows what that vampire had us doing?" she said with a ghost of a stammer.

"Oh, dang it. It's just a zit. How disappointing," I teased.

"You...you...bitches!" she barked, clamping her hand over her mouth. "No. I'm not sorry I said that. Even if it adds extra time on getting some frickin' angel wings, I'm still not sorry."

"Oh, we love you too," I replied. "The good news is that Ash can't be a vampire, or he wouldn't have been able to control his appetite. Surely he would have wanted our blood."

Chloe rubbed her neck, still upset by my little prank. "Then he was probably too full after sucking the juices out of Mary and Kathy, and who knows who else!"

"If that's the case, then he's hardly the insatiable vampire described in your romance novels. Maybe Ash suffers from fang dysfunction." Jade shrugged.

"Fine. Joke all you want. But you have to admit Ash meets all the minimum requirements. He's practically prequalified to be a vampire! Just remember how spooky it was the day he showed up. So, despite not knowing about his mind powers, his taste for blood, or his sexual prowess, he is still my number one suspect."

"And who is the runner up on your list?" I asked.

"Zane, of course."

"Oh, please. If Zane is a vampire, he sure has been hiding it well," I replied.

"And that's the only reason he is in second place. Anyway, don't worry about it. Jade and I have your back. Right, Jade?"

"Uh, yeah," Jade mumbled, obviously caught off-guard by Chloe's ever-expanding list of vampire suspects.

Of course, I dismissed it. There was no way my hot-blooded boyfriend could be a cold, clammy vampire.

By the afternoon, I caught myself remembering the day

Ash showed up. At one point, I even conferred with Harry which gave me a brief respite.

"Aha! No way can Ash be a vampire. We never invited him inside."

But minutes later, I caught a glimpse of our flag fluttering in the wind, welcoming customers to 'Come On In!" Surely any cunning vampire would consider that an invitation based on a technicality.

The more I thought about it, the more unnerved I became—to the point of feeling downright queasy. I hated to admit it, but Chloe was right. Ash's mysterious arrival amidst a sudden storm was spooky for sure. But she was dead wrong about Zane.

CHAPTER THREE

"Sorry, closing time," Chloe said, shutting the door on Zane. "Come back tomorrow."

Nudging her aside, I grabbed his arm and pulled him in.

"Please disregard her. She scared herself this morning."

"Scared about?" he asked.

"She's got this crazy idea that you might be—ouch!" Chloe stomped on my foot.

"That you might be contagious," she said, finishing my sentence.

"Contagious? With what?" he asked.

"Whooping cough, measles, cholera, how should I know?" Chloe mumbled, walking away.

"Seriously, Zane, never mind her." Frankly, I was done overthinking Mary and Kathy's predicaments and Chloe's suspicions. I needed a break, even if it was just until the next day.

"Have any plans this afternoon and evening?" I asked, hopeful he didn't have anything on his calendar.

"Funny you should ask. Because I do have plans, with you.

There's a place I'd like to show you, but it requires a swimsuit. Are you in?"

"Of course. Just give me a minute," I raced upstairs to my room.

Feeling somewhat courageous, I changed into a brandnew, hot pink bikini. I have to admit, it showed a bit more skin than I was used to, but it was similar to the swimsuits girls my age wore. To me, it felt more like being caught in public in nothing more than my bra and underwear.

I was still on the fence about the whole bikini thing, but I wanted to spend the afternoon with Zane, and apparently today's activities required a swimsuit.

Covering up with a light summer dress, I quickly returned downstairs. Chloe and Jade were busy lurking in the shadows, undoubtedly observing Zane for the slightest hint of vampiric behavior.

Silly girls. It was a perfectly sunny day, and we all knew vampires were allergic to sun.

I held on tight to Zane as we sped out of town, wishing I'd opted for pants instead of a dress. As I'd quickly found out, a light summer dress was not the best outfit for riding on the back of Zane's motorcycle.

Our trip inland caught me off guard. I'd assumed we would be heading to the beach. Open fields and pastures were replaced by trees until we slowed and turned down a narrow gravel road. The road—if you could call it that—was not much more than a trail that twisted through a thick dark forest and walls of moss-covered cliffs. It was beautiful and spooky at the same time.

Once we finally came to a stop and parked the motorcycle, I tried to maintain some semblance of modesty as I awkwardly hopped off the back of the bike.

Remind me to never wear a dress again when traveling on the back of Zane's bike.

We walked hand in hand along a short narrow path which led us to the most amazing hidden gem. We stood on the border of the rocky outcropping, which was about ten feet above an open, bowl shaped glen. To our right, a stream cascaded out of the forest and over the rocky edge. The crystal-clear water formed a wide, but delicately thin veil as it dropped into a deep blue pond below. It was truly the most beautiful waterfall I'd ever seen.

"Well? What do you think of it?" Zane asked.

"It's absolutely beautiful. All of it," I said, awed by the scene.

"This is just one of many truly magical places in this area."

"Now I can fully understand why your mom and the Hellions have been so determined to protect this natural beauty from development."

"Oh, it's more than just the beauty of it. For them, each special place has a hidden magic—a kind of magic that only beings with a supernatural origin can unlock."

"Ah, I see. So, since your father is a devil and your mom a witch, is that good enough for you to unlock it?"

I wondered if he'd finally explain to me what his secret nature was.

"Of course. And since you were created by angels, I'm betting you can too. But first..."

He kissed me.

"First, we have to get rid of these clothes."

I tried not to pout as Zane stepped away from me and our kiss. My pout instantly disappeared when he started to undress. Thankfully, he didn't stop until he wore nothing but his swimming trunks.

I tried to look away, I really did. But my eyes were glued to his body, watching every move he made with wicked fascination.

I'd imagined stripping off my dress in the most sexy and

seductive manner possible, giving Zane the same viewing pleasure he'd given me. Instead, like the dork I am, I blushed and awkwardly fumbled with the material. Zane stepped forward and kissed me again. His hands moved quickly, and before I realized what he was doing, the dress crumpled around my feet.

"You look beautiful," he whispered.

I blushed even more and tried not to cover myself with my hands. I wasn't ashamed of my body, but it was a bit unnerving to feel so exposed.

"Ready?" he asked, holding my hand.

I didn't know for sure where he was going with his question. "Well, I'm not sure. You see, I'm—"

"Three, two, one! Jump!" he shouted.

As we leapt from the edge, I braced myself for the plunge into the icy spring-fed pond. I expected to feel thousands of tiny needles stabbing into my skin as we hit the water, but the expected shock from the frigid water never hit me.

How weird.

Instead, the water was as warm as a bath. When I broke through the surface and opened my eyes, the shady forest glen had been magically transformed into a lush tropical oasis in the middle of the cool northern forest. Dew-covered ferns which previously crowded the shore had been replaced by huge, brightly colored flowers. The dark-branched evergreens shifted into sun dappled palms.

Swimming through the blue crystal water, I joined Zane on a rock ledge next to the waterfall. "You weren't kidding when you said this place was magic. It's absolutely amazing."

"It's one of my favorite spots. Not all of these magical places are as welcoming. Some of them are downright weird. Just promise me that you and your friends won't try to find them on your own. It would be fine if you were all mortal humans, but...for people like us, they also act as doorways."

"Doorways?" I asked.

"Yeah. Openings or passages the Hellions use to travel to and from another dimension."

"You mean Hell," I said matter of factly.

"Sure, okay, Hell. Maybe that is one name for a certain place. But how would you describe Heaven? Can you simply limit your description to your house, your street, your neighborhood?"

"I suppose you are right. I've only been to certain sectors of Heaven. But I know it's a far more complex place, with multiple worlds, in different dimensions. At least, that's what my parents have told me."

"Well, the same goes for Hell, and the other dimensions in between. I haven't traveled to many, but I have to tell you there are an infinite number of worlds we could explore. But as for me, I like it here, at home, on Earth. Maybe I feel most at home here because this is the point where Heaven and Hell meet."

"I always considered my life in Heaven to be a happy one, but I was never quite content. Everyone could tell. It made me kind of a misfit around Heaven, as you can imagine. It wasn't until I came to this world, the mortal world, in between dimensions that I've learned what was missing."

"And...what was it you were missing?"

Oh gosh, how to explain it...

I took a minute to sort out my thoughts. I didn't want to make it sound like Heaven was a bad place, because it wasn't. It was a true paradise.

When I finally started to speak, the words flew from my mouth without any afterthought.

"Things like...when you're looking forward to a sunny day at the beach, but the weather has been cold and rainy all week. Or when you absolutely crave a pepperoni pizza, but the pizza place is closed. And then, every once in a while, you get that pizza and a perfect day on the beach."

"Ah, so you were spoiled up there in Heaven, but denial has taught you to appreciate the things you enjoy. I'm not sure it's opposite of the Hellions, but it is an interesting comparison."

"What? How so?" I asked.

How could he compare angels to demons?

"In their case, they were locked in Hell and denied any worldly pleasures. But here, they've gotten a taste of all those worldly pleasures, and now they've completely adopted the classical hedonistic philosophy."

"So, they think it's virtuous to indulge in drunken orgies and whatever earthly pleasure crosses their perverted minds? Not to sound too snooty or angelic, but self-destructive behavior doesn't seem like a very ethical philosophy to me."

"Ethics are relative anyway, but I don't think the word 'ethical' is even in their vocabulary. As far as they're concerned, happiness comes from finding pleasure. Simple, selfish and childish. But they sure know how to throw a party."

"And what about you? What is so interesting about this world that keeps you here? If it's true what you said about this forest, there are all kinds of rabbit holes you could pop in and out of," I asked.

"Look around you. See how the sun penetrates through the green palm fronds, into the blue glassy depths of the pond? See the water grasses waving in the current? And how the rocks and logs look like the wreck of a sunken treasure ship? It's like it's urging me on to see the deeper, hidden beauty in things," he said, peering into the water.

"And as I discover the surprises hidden all around us, I'm driven to see more. I could spend a lifetime traveling just this world. And above it all is the anticipation of finding what is waiting. There is plenty here. Especially right in front of me."

"It really turns me on when you get all Steinbeckian on me," I teased, pushing him backward onto a grassy bed.

"Yeah? I happen to be working on my own book about my adventures. Gonna call it Travels with Emmy," he teased.

"Like I'm your pet, I see." I lightly traced the shape of a heart on his bare chest. "I hope I'm more than that."

"Remember what I said about anticipation?" he whispered.

"And remember what I said about wanting something more?" I replied, bringing my lips to meet his kiss.

Our bodies intertwined, our bare skin pressing against each other. It would have been so easy, and it felt so right to surrender to his touch right then and there.

"Just...there's just something I need to know." I panted.

"What are you? I mean, really? Who are you? Devil for a father, witch for a mother...is there more to you than I know? My friends seem to think so. They've been frantically waving caution flags like I'm squealing around a racetrack with no brakes and my engine on fire."

Zane didn't answer right away. He stayed silent just long enough for me to worry that I'd struck a nerve. I let out a sigh of relief when he calmly replied.

"Understandable, given the circumstances. We are, in fact, having this discussion in the middle of an enchanted forest. And other circumstances, like the fact that your beautiful and nearly naked body is pressed against me. It makes me wonder if the mystery surrounding me kind of turns you on."

His upturned hand lightly traced a path from my chest down to my stomach. I fully expected him to stop just as he reached my bikini bottoms, but he didn't. His light, teasing touch continued on until I felt his fingertips brush ever so lightly over my sex.

Instant blush.

"Kinda," I whispered.

Dang it! He's right about his mysteriousness adding to his hotness. If he only knew what really drives me wild—that he's the opposite of what any good angel should desire. I've got to turn this around.

My blush subsiding, I took a matter-of-fact tone. "Sure, you're mysterious and all. Pretty hot too."

Forcing my hand to stop trembling, I turned his actions around and took a page out of his playbook. I allowed my hand to roam his bare chest in almost the exact pattern his hand had traveled on me.

I should have done the angelic thing and stopped when I reached the fabric of his swimsuit, but I didn't. I allowed my fingers to brush over the noticeable bulge in his shorts.

"But you can't hide the fact that I'm the one turning you on. Apparently, my angelic sexiness is just too much for you to handle."

I kissed him before he could answer.

Honestly, it was too much for me. Another ten seconds, I'd have torn both of our swimsuits off. Without warning, I slipped back into the water and swam as deep and far as I could. And you know what? I wasn't anxious, worried, or frightened if Zane had some sort of sinister beast lurking within.

Like a novice fire dancer who successfully performed the dangerous art of twirling fiery batons without becoming a human torch, I felt confident and pretty darn proud of myself. I walked, I mean swam, away from my sexy partial demon with my dignity intact.

Not bad for a vulnerable virgin angel who'd just committed her first overtly sexual act—if you can call it that.

Just as I rose to the surface, I caught a glimpse of something bright at the bottom of the pond. It reminded me of the way a diamond might twinkle in the sun—but with even more brilliance. After filling my lungs with fresh air, I dove down. Hoping to find the remarkable jewel, I scanned the sandy floor.

Nothing.

By the time I resurfaced, Zane was sitting upright, smiling sexily. Obviously, he enjoyed watching me swim back to the rocky ledge.

"Did you lose something down there?" he asked.

"No. I spotted something shimmering at the bottom of the pond. It looked like a jewel, but I'm not sure. So, I went back for another look but couldn't find anything."

"It's probably for the best. I forgot to tell you the most important rule about these magical places. You can't take anything out. Ever."

"Why is that?"

"I'm not sure why. All I know is that I've been warned over and over."

"And you've never once tested that rule? You're not such a rebel after all," I teased.

"Meh. Just a smart rebel. I don't want to end up with an incurable curse."

"Curse?" I asked, seriously hoping he had a punchline waiting. "Do you really mean that?"

"Yeah, I do. Ever since I was a kid, my mom warned me about it. So did the Hellions. And they were dead serious. There are things in every alternate dimension that appear to be one thing, but they become something entirely different when moved to the Earthly realm. Something beautiful becomes something sinister. It's a price you pay for upsetting the balance. I don't know the specific punishment, but I've never been interested in finding out firsthand. Anyway, the sun will be setting soon. We should get out of here," he said, handing me a towel.

His tone was somber, and his ominous warning was

enough to dissipate what remained of the sexually charged atmosphere.

Returning to his motorcycle, I noticed the magical glen had reverted back to the dark forest pond. I'll admit, it gave me goosebumps.

Wrapping my arms around him, I held on tightly as we sped away from our magical date. By the time we returned to the shop, my fears were replaced by my newly found confidence in touching Zane—in ways I'd previously been too shy to attempt. I knew we'd both stepped up another rung on our physical relationship, and I was fine with it.

Zane was being more than patient with me, and I resolved myself to set up an ultimate and climactic date at the earliest opportunity—on my own terms of course.

CHAPTER FOUR

"*W*ell?" Jade asked.

"Oh my God. You will not believe what happened or what I did! We went swimming in a magical pond and made out. It was hot. So hot. I think he's the one. I'm finally ready."

"What?" Chloe yipped like an angry chihuahua. "You were supposed to question him about vampires, demons with hypnotic powers, or what other sort of devilish beast could be behind the rash of mind-controlling blackmail schemes. We really don't want to hear about your sexual adventures."

"The hell we don't!" Jade replied. "Let's hear it!"

"All right. I guess I want to hear about it too. But why didn't you interrogate Zane?"

"Probably because her mouth was otherwise occupied," Jade replied, jabbing her elbow into Chloe's side.

"Umm...you're absolutely right, Chloe. I was completely distracted and forgot all about the mystery we were working on."

"Well," Chloe sighed. "I actually would like to compare

boy notes. I think I might be getting to that same point with my feelings for Daryl."

"You guys are giving me hope," Jade added.

"We can talk about it later. Even though I didn't talk to Zane about the situation, I did find out why the forest is so important to Eve and the Hellions. The swimming hole we went to was just a spring in the woods, but once we got closer, it magically transformed into a beautiful tropical pool."

"So, they like swimming?" Chloe asked.

"I guess, but it's more than that. Zane said there are dozens of places hidden in that forest. He called them magical portals. The one he took me to transformed into a tropical oasis, but the others open into all different sorts of dimensions. He described them as portals that the Hellions can use to move between dimensions."

"So, demons get magical portals to tropical swimming pools? Jeez. And to think we got dropped out of Heaven like yesterday's trash. I'm starting to think we're on the wrong team," Jade said.

"Well, I wouldn't trade in your halo for horns just yet. Zane told me that not all those portals are as nice as the one he took me to."

"That makes sense." Chloe nodded. "If the Hellions are hopping through them, going back and forth between dimensions, they're actually demonic doorways. I can just imagine how scary some of those might turn out to be. Who knows, maybe that magical pool he took you to was something more sinister than you realized. How are you feeling?" she asked, leaning close as if she was examining me for diabolical changes to my very soul.

"Nah, she's fine. Horny and frustrated, but fine," Jade teased.

Pushing her aside, I dismissed her comment. "Let's get

back to the mystery at hand. If we really want to live up to our expectations, we need to figure out who is blackmailing our friends. Honestly, what are your thoughts?"

"Forget mind controlling vampires or whatever, I'm going to say it's hypnosis. I saw a show on TV last week where the hypnotist convinced a volunteer she was a chicken. With a snap of his finger, she started clucking around the stage. Whoever is doing this is using the same trick."

"Hypnosis? I don't know about that. Possibly, but someone with those skills in this little town? He or she would've used it for entertainment, like a magic show. They'd be really well-known around here and we would've heard about it."

Jade shrugged. "So, if it's not a supernatural being or a hypnotist, what's your guess?"

"Some kind of drug. You know, something they could slip into a drink to make a person forget? I don't really know."

"No way," Chloe said. "If it were a drug, those women would've been passed out cold in those pictures. I'm sticking with my vampire theory. And that vampire is Ash, the stranger from the storm."

The jingling bells on our store's front door interrupted our conversation.

"Well, hello, Officer Daryl. What brings you here this evening? Official police business?" Chloe asked, adjusting her thick glasses and leaning her tiny frame against the counter.

It was such an awkward pose. For a few seconds, I wondered if she was contorted into a weird shape as a result of a severe back spasm.

Daryl was dressed in his usual freshly pressed uniform, tailored extremely tight to show off his fit body.

"That's right, ma'am. I have a few questions for you," Daryl said, forcing a stern and deep tone.

Chloe sauntered toward him. "Oh my. Will you be taking me into...custody?" she asked, dramatically spinning around.

"What the hell is going on?" I whispered into Jade's ear.

"They've been doing this weird role play kink thing. It's hilarious, actually," she whispered back. "Just watch."

"Yes, ma'am. Or is it Scarlet Panther?" he asked, taking out his handcuffs. "But first, I'll need to frisk you down," he said, quite seriously, before he temporarily slipped out of his role and whispered to her. "Hey, you wanna go upstairs first, Chloe?"

"Please take the Scarlet Panther upstairs. We've seen enough," I groaned.

I barely got the words out before they were racing up the stairs, presumably to Chloe's room.

"They're cute. Weird, but cute," Jade said.

Intending to give our friends as much privacy as we could, Jade and I stepped out on the porch to enjoy the evening air and some hot chocolate.

After five minutes of sipping our hot drinks, Jade broke the silence. "So...things are really heating up between you and Zane?"

"Definitely. I just...I know I'm an adult and free to do what I want. I just hope I know what I'm doing. How is a prospective angel supposed to act? I keep wondering if this is all a test."

Jade replied with a little shrug. "Maybe."

Nodding toward a cozy looking couple strolling down the sidewalk, she asked, "Do you think it's any different for the regular, everyday people? You're a sincere person, Emmy. I think all three of us are. Handing your heart over to someone else's care is serious business. It leaves you so vulnerable. That's where trust comes in. So, if you believe you can trust him with your heart, go for it. That's just my opinion. Take it for what it's worth."

"You're wise beyond your years," I replied, halfway teasingly. "And what about the Scarlet Panther upstairs? You think she's already...you know?"

"Nah, she would've told us. I believe they're both rounding third base though, with their kinky little games. Our ignorance has been catching up to us."

"How so?"

"Well, the other evening Erik and I, along with Daryl and Chloe went for a walk on the beach. When we asked them if we could give them hand jobs, it was then we found out that it didn't mean holding hands while strolling in the moonlight."

"Gurk!" I choked on my drink. "Oh my God, Jade. You didn't."

"Imagine our surprise once they took us behind the boathouse, and we found out what it really meant."

"Awkward," I mumbled.

"Other than Chloe talking the whole time, I'd say it turned out more messy than awkward."

"Oh, geez," I whispered, rubbing my forehead.

We resumed sipping our drinks in silence, watching the stars appear as twilight faded. I had no words. And I refused to share any secrets of my recent steamy make-out sessions with Zane.

In the distance, an ambulance's siren pierced the air. Upstairs, Chloe's shouts for help carried out from the balcony.

"I can't find it! Help!"

Ditching our cozy chairs, we bolted upstairs. You can imagine our shock when we entered Chloe's room. Daryl was bare-chested, seated in a chair. His hands were cuffed behind his back. Thankfully, he was still in his boxers. The only clothes Chloe had on were her skimpy thong panties and

Daryl's police shirt, which hung on her like an open robe. His police officer's hat sat cockeyed on her head.

A radio squawked its repeated calls for Daryl. Glancing toward the source, I found it on the bed, buried under Chloe's bra and Daryl's pants. I held the button and replied, "Just a second! I'll get him!"

Holding it close to Daryl, I once again keyed the microphone. "Got it, Betty! Be there in a minute," he shouted.

"It's a 911 call for an ambulance down at Mike Schmitz's place. Someone found him unconscious by his front door."

Jade joined Chloe in her search for the keys. "This is beyond awkward, Scarlet Panther," she complained.

Chloe dropped to her hands and knees. "My very first lap dance and the radio starts squawking. Then the keys! The damned handcuff keys, I dropped them somewhere."

Instinctively wanting to help with the 911 emergency, I headed for the door. Shouting over my shoulder, "I know where that is. It's only two blocks away, I'll see if I can help!"

I wasn't exactly sure how I could be of assistance. But hey, some angelic intervention couldn't hurt. Right?

The ambulance was already on the scene by the time I made it. The paramedic just happened to be Jade's rescuer and boyfriend, Erik. Wiggling through the small crowd of gawkers, I was shocked to see Erik pull a sheet over poor deceased Mike Schmitz. Even if there would've been something I could've done, I was too late.

Daryl, apparently freed from the Scarlet Panther's erotic restraints, arrived on the scene. "What happened?" he asked.

"Can't say for sure. But from what several witnesses described, he showed classic signs of a massive heart attack. The coroner will know pretty quickly."

I listened in while Daryl questioned witnesses and got the whole story. Mike had walked up to his front door, took out his key and suddenly dropped a coffee cup while clutching his chest. He collapsed and never regained consciousness.

The little crowd quietly dispersed as the ambulance disappeared into the night.

Jade and Chloe finally joined me on the scene, and I broke the sad news.

"I saw the guy around town. He always seemed like a gentleman," Jade said.

"Yeah. I saw him too. I don't like to talk bad about the dead, but the only time I'd heard him speak was a few weeks ago. He was yelling at a group of people who were taking pictures at the beach. Something about their evil cell phones. He was really angry about the use of technology. A few of the people called him a crazy old man and kept snapping pictures."

"Weird," I mumbled, staring at the building where Mike died. I was certain I'd walked past this building a million times and had never noticed the shield-shaped patch next to the door. The color of the patch didn't quite match the rest of the siding.

"Daryl, do you know why this is here?" I asked.

"Oh, that. The mark was left by a sign from an old business Mr. Schmitz used to have."

"Business? What was it?"

"A photography studio. In the past, he did a lot of portraits for graduations, weddings, and such. But I think most of his business was selling photographs to the tourists. He closed shop a few years ago. I guess business slowed down, and he was getting close to retiring anyway." Daryl shrugged.

Turning to Chloe, he took her hand in his. "Sorry, but I've got some paperwork to take care of now. See you tomorrow sometime?"

"Of course," she replied before kissing him goodbye.

"Did you hear that? He was a photographer. Had I known, he would've been my number one suspect in our blackmail cases," I said, too excited to keep my voice at a whisper.

"Huh?" Jade asked, her expression contorted with bewilderment. "What does photography have to do with mind control?"

"All of those photos look like they were done by a professional. The setting, the lighting, the poses...they were magazine quality," I reminded her.

"Ah." Chloe nodded, as if she agreed with me for once. "So, you think Mike Schmitz was the vampire? Then he wouldn't truly be dead, unless someone drove a stake through his heart, of course. Which he wasn't staked. So, what do vampires and photographers have in common?"

I had to take a deep breath. As loveable as Chloe is, sometimes, she made me want to rip my hair out.

"No, Chloe, I never said he was a vampire. I'm just saying that all of those pictures were taken by a professional photographer. And just maybe, he found a way to control his victims. Even though he's dead, he's our number one suspect."

"If that's true, it's case closed. His victims have nothing more to worry about," Jade said.

"Quite possibly. Still, we need to be sure. And part of that is figuring out how he could have brainwashed those women. And our first step is getting inside. I heard witnesses tell Daryl that Mike was getting his key out just before he collapsed. I bet it's laying around here someplace."

"Great. Another key to find." Jade bent down for a better look. "Come on, Scarlet Panther, back on your knees."

"Hush," Chloe growled.

Surprisingly, the key was on the ground right in front of the door, next to Mike's discarded coffee cup.

"There it is!" I announced.

"Into the vampire's lair." Chloe picked up the key and

attempted to unlock the door. "That's weird. It's already unlocked."

"We all had assumed Mike was arriving at his studio when he'd had a heart attack. It's more likely he was leaving and about to lock up when he collapsed."

Chloe took the lead, entering the dark studio. "Keep an eye out, just in case there's a whole nest of vampires."

"One in a gazillion," I mumbled what I figured the odds were of Mike being a semi-retired photographer and full-time vampire.

Timidly following her through the door, I felt a chill run up my back. "Hold up, Chloe! If we turn the lights on and start nosing around, everyone in town is going to know we're in here. It seems like it would be awfully suspicious for us to be in here snooping about. We should come back in the morning and sneak in when it's daylight, so we can have a proper look around the place," I said, hoping I was being logical and not just being a big chicken.

"Good thinking. Plus, it'll give me time to put together a proper vampire hunting kit. Just like they used in the Dark Beasts, book seventeen."

"Oh yeah, Staken not Stirred. Loved that one," I replied.

Retreating from the studio, Chloe locked the door. "But we have to be back here at first light," she said, double checking the lock.

CHAPTER FIVE

I wasn't sure how serious Chloe was about her vampire theory. You just never know with her. But when she met us on our front porch with a backpack bristling with pointy wooden sticks, I knew she meant business.

"You look like you're smuggling a porcupine. What else do you have jammed in there?" Jade asked, peering into the bag.

"A hammer, of course. We didn't have any fresh garlic cloves, so I grabbed a container of garlic powder from the spice rack. And an old pickle jar I filled with holy water from the baptismal pool at the church up on the hill. I even have a little cross made of genuine silver. I'm not sure if silver works on vampires or just werewolves, but I figure it can't hurt to have an extra layer of protection. You know what I mean?"

"Absolutely. It's better to be safe than sorry when it comes to vampires!" Jade replied, obviously faking her sincerity. "But you know, I've given this whole vampire thing some thought. If even one vampire was hunting in Angel Bay, wouldn't we have victims? Like bodies drained of blood, fang marks in the neck, the usual kind of thing?"

"Not at all," Chloe scoffed. "The vampires I've read about are always inconspicuous. Besides hypnotizing their victims, they bite them very discreetly...and sensually...right here," she said, lifting the hem of her shorts and pointing to her inner thigh. "They wouldn't be as obvious as the ones in those cheesy Hollywood movies."

"Ah, of course." Jade turned in my direction and rolled her eyes.

"And we have to be especially wary when it comes to vampires. Our blood would be considered top shelf, being that we're practically angels, and because we're still virgins. We're all still virgins, right?"

"We are, but I think we were wondering about you, Scarlet Panther," I said.

"Trust me, things have been getting heated, but we haven't gone as far as you might think." Chloe adjusted her glasses. "More or less. An angel has to consider her reputation, after all."

"We better get moving before too many people are out and about. It will make sneaking into the studio all the more difficult, if not downright impossible," I said, glancing up at the rising sun.

Arriving at the studio, we were immediately on high alert. The front door that we'd carefully locked the night before was ajar. Although the door, and the handle, didn't appear to have any visible damage, the deadbolt had been sheared off.

"How does something like this even happen?" Jade poked at what remained of the deadbolt. "It looks...melted. Like someone cut right through it with a torch, but there aren't any burn marks on the door or the frame."

It was obvious the place had been broken into after we had left the previous night, and in a highly creative way.

Chloe quickly readied a sharpened stake and a hammer while I simply called out, "Hello? Is anyone here?"

The studio was dead silent and had been completely ransacked.

Someone had certainly broken in overnight, and they had been searching for something specific.

"It wasn't a burglary. All the expensive camera equipment is still here," I said. "My guess is that whoever did this also suspected Mike of the blackmail scheme, and they were looking to get rid of any compromising information. It could be a partner in crime, or it could be a victim. Let's spread out and have a look around."

"What exactly is it that we are looking for, specifically?" Jade asked.

"We're looking for clues. Anything that will link Mike with the blackmail scheme, also any drugs or other evidence of mind control. And maybe clues that will help us figure out who broke in overnight," I said.

It didn't take us long to find what we were looking for. After about twenty minutes of rummaging through the studio, Jade found an unlocked cash box containing four thousand dollars in large bills. "This was definitely not a burglary," she said, replacing the money.

Chloe eyed up a recently painted patch on the wall. Chiseling at the drywall with a wooden vampire stake, she discovered a hidden cavity.

"Here we go!" Chloe said, removing a stack of glossy photos. Squinting, she studied them from different angles. "I wonder if mine looks like that. I sure hope not. Oh wow, this woman's vagina looks like Chewbacca got punched in the mouth. What the heck is wrong with this one? It's completely bald. Yikes! Here's another one that doesn't have a hair on her."

"Oh my god! Here's a picture of Kathy. And all the rest of these...they are all pictures of other women in town," Jade said.

"We definitely solved the mystery of who was behind the camera. I say we destroy every one of these photos," she added, dropping them into a paper shredder and flipping the switch to on.

"Now we just have to figure out how he did it." I rifled through a desk drawer stuffed with slips of miscellaneous papers. A familiar looking receipt stood out among the mess.

"What's this? It's a sales receipt from our store. I don't ever remember him coming into the shop. Do either of you?"

"No," Chloe and Jade said at the same time.

"Is there a date on the receipt?" Jade asked.

I scanned the receipt. "It's dated from over a year ago, when Midge was still the owner. One antique book, titled Le Dragon Rouge. Condition as-is, and the price was five hundred dollars." I read the receipt out loud.

"Interesting. I think we know what Mike's motivation was. He blackmailed women for money since his business was failing. And it appears to have worked. But why buy an antique book for so much money? It doesn't appear he was a collector. At least, I certainly haven't seen any antiques in here," Jade said.

"I wonder where that book is now?" Chloe asked.

Splitting up once more, we resumed our search. After ten minutes, I was about to call it quits.

Chloe's shrieks suddenly reverberated through the studio, making me nearly jump out of my shoes. It was clear she came across something horrific. I was afraid we had somehow ended up with another dead body on our hands.

Jade and I raced down the corridor toward her cries. Turning the corner, we found Chloe standing in front of an empty cage. And when I say cage, I don't mean a birdcage. It was big, like an old-time jail cell. The iron door appeared to have been nearly ripped from its hinges. Whatever had been kept in that cage was on the loose.

Chloe's face was ghostly white. Her hands trembled, her fingers wrapping tightly around one of the wooden stakes.

"What sort of monster do you think was in here?" she whispered, which seemed kind of pointless since she'd already screamed like a scalded banshee.

Jade stepped inside the cage and glanced around. "Hmmm. There's an old ripped up mattress for a bed. A couple of empty bowls, presumably for food and water. Could've been a large dog."

I joined her inside and immediately noticed several deep gouges in the cinderblock wall. They looked like giant claw marks. Clearly, they were made by some sort of animal, but I had no idea what kind of animal had claws that large. "Check out these claw marks. They're massive. This was no dog. Maybe he kept a lion or a tiger in here?"

"Or a vampire. Who knows? I have no desire to find out," Chloe mumbled, tracing her fingers over the door's twisted iron bars.

"I agree. We should get out of here. At least we've learned enough to prove Mike was the one behind the blackmailing, even if we don't know how he pulled it off."

Leaving the studio, I spotted Mike's discarded paper cup on the ground, right where he dropped it when he collapsed. Despite his repulsive behavior, or maybe because of it, I felt a sudden twinge of sadness for him.

"What a way to waste your life—hurting the people of your community." I picked up the cup and jammed it into Chloe's backpack with the intent of throwing it away when we got home.

Jade shielded her eyes from the rising sun. "It's still early. How about we swing by Kathy's for coffee and donuts. We can break the good news to her in person. Uhh—not that someone's death should be good news, but you know what I mean."

47

Wiggling the sharpened stake into its place in her back-pack, Chloe glanced at her bag. "This whole situation still bugs me. It sure is weird, the way whoever it was broke into Mike's studio. Hey, do you think someone broke in, to free whatever was in that cage? Or was it the creature from the cage who had ripped the front door open to get out?"

"We'll probably never know, but either theory is possible," I said, doing my best to conceal my fears of what sort of beast could be roaming Angel Bay. "We need to tell Daryl that a wild animal could be on the loose."

Jade stopped in her tracks. "No way! You can't be serious. Imagine what kind of trouble we'll be in for trespassing."

"These people are our neighbors and friends, Jade. It's our duty to protect them. Even if it means that we find ourselves in trouble in order to help them."

"This sounds like a job for the Scarlet Panther," Chloe said, cheerfully.

"I'll just tell Daryl that we were passing by and saw the door open. We took a peek inside to see if someone was in there, and when we did, we saw the mess and the open cage. He doesn't need to know everything we're up to. If he starts asking too many questions, I can distract him with some of those new poses I learned from those uhh—pictures we saw this morning."

"Poor Daryl," Jade said, crossing the street to Kathy's.

"Such beautiful flowers," I said, walking the path through Kathy's flower garden.

Kathy's bakery was already in its busiest hour. While Chloe and Jade kept the girl behind the counter occupied by ordering our coffee and donuts, I managed to pull Kathy aside. "I don't know if you heard the tragic news. Mike Schmitz passed away last night."

"Oh my gosh. I had no idea he was even ill."

"Just so you know, we think he was the individual who

was blackmailing you, and the others. We snuck into his studio this morning and found a stash of compromising pictures, including some of you. We shredded all of the pictures we found, so you never have to worry about this again."

"Thank you so much, Emmy. Do you know how he was able to hypnotize me or whatever he did?"

"Unfortunately, no. But I guess it doesn't matter now, due to last night's unfortunate coincidence."

"No, I suppose it doesn't. Thanks again for being so discreet."

I wondered if I should warn her about a possible vicious tiger or bear at large, but I figured that sort of news would best be left to an official, like Daryl.

Walking home, I thought about the strange cage, the melted deadbolt, and the proof of Mike Schmitz's guilt. I wanted everything to make sense, if you will. That way, I could place all of my thoughts into a neat little package and not worry about it anymore—call it case closed, mystery solved, or whatever. But, of course, it was all too weird. The entire situation was strange. There were too many unanswered questions for me to be able to box things up in my mind, and there was something off about my very short conversation with Kathy that didn't sit right. I just couldn't put my finger on what it was.

I was glad to be back at the shop, with my mind pleasantly occupied by curious tourists. By early afternoon, I stopped to chat with Chloe after she returned from a lunch date with Daryl.

"So, Chloe, what did Daryl think?"

"Uh—I don't know," she stammered. "I—I felt...awkward about the whole thing. I couldn't pose like I'd talked about. I thought I could, but it was just a bit too bold and straightforward, even for me. I'm sorry. I couldn't go through with it."

"No, silly. I meant about the cage—the claw marks. What does he think of it?"

"Oh, yeah. We stopped by and I showed it to him. He seemed more concerned with the way the place had been turned inside out. But he did say he would call someone from the county animal control to check it out. Either way, we can't go back there. He told me that he's treating it as a crime scene—because of the breaking and entering at the very least."

"He wasn't even a little bit concerned with the cage?"

"Not really," she sighed.

"He lacks imagination. With him, everything has to have a logical explanation. I mean, I've considered that whatever was in that cage could've been a monster, a captive vampire, a dragon even. But noooo. According to Daryl, he's never seen anything supernatural, therefore, it can't exist," she huffed, obviously disappointed. "Maybe he isn't the right guy for me after all."

"Um. Maybe he's exactly the kind of guy you need to keep your wonderfully active imagination from kicking into overdrive."

"Really? You think so?"

I did think so. Daryl and Chloe were so cute together and absolutely perfect. I didn't want Chloe to doubt her relationship just because Daryl was fully human and didn't understand the absolute truth that supernatural beings existed, and they were all around him.

"As long as he's respectful of your opinions and doesn't just dismiss everything you say out of hand."

"I suppose he listens to my opinions, even if he doesn't really believe in them."

"Hey kids," Jade said, wedging herself between us. "You're talking about guys again, aren't you?"

"Just one, and his name is Daryl," Chloe replied.

"Perfect timing. Erik just called me and invited me to a fundraising get-together the first responders are holding this Friday evening. Did Daryl ask you to go?"

"Yep. We talked about it over lunch."

"So, are you going?"

"Of course. It means I'll get to spend more time with Daryl."

"Good. Then I'll have someone to hang out with when the men transform into boys and do whatever it is they're supposed to do at this fundraising thing."

"I feel like we're going to be ditching Emmy now," Chloe sighed.

"Oh, not at all." I didn't even have to fake my enthusiasm. I haven't really had much alone time since our arrival in Angel Bay. But the thought of having the apartment all to myself on a Friday night? A plan was already starting to hatch in my head.

"I don't have any plans with Zane, but I could sure use a nice, quiet evening at home. You guys go out and have a great time."

"Uh huh," Jade mumbled, giving me a side-eyed look. "Home alone."

"Why not?" I said, unable to conceal my smile.

CHAPTER SIX

inally, Friday night! Jade and Chloe were out on their double date with Daryl and Erik, and I had our upstairs apartment all to myself.

Like a spider spinning her web, I'd made my plans. This was it. I was ready to surf that wave a little closer to the rocks. All the way, in fact, and on my terms.

To Zane's surprise, I turned down his offer for a night out on the town and countered with my own offer of staying in and having dinner at home.

My heart raced at the thought of what I had planned.

"Perfect," I mumbled, lighting the last of a half dozen candles which I'd carefully arranged for the perfect ambience. Checking the mirror, I teased my blonde hair over my shoulders and quickly adjusted my sleeveless little black cocktail dress. It was cut short. So short, in fact, I was ashamed to ever wear it in public.

But for this one occasion, it was the ideal outfit. It was truly symbolic. Because this was it, the big night. For the longest time, I'd made this huge deal about my first time, and how it might tarnish my proverbial halo.

But at twenty-two years old, I was way beyond that point. I mean way, way beyond it. I was not only ready to get it out of the way, I was also ready to jump in and enjoy it.

A formerly frozen pepperoni pizza was fresh out of the oven, and the table was set. I opened a bottle of cherry wine, which looked much better than it smelled. I held my breath and choked down a glass. I really didn't like the taste of wine. I'd only bought it because I was hoping it would help me relax. I may have been mentally prepared for the evening I'd planned, but I was still as jumpy as a frog in a frying pan.

Zane arrived at six o'clock on the dot. He was right on time. My punctual demon—I mean, punctual partial demon.

"Come in." I greeted him at the door.

Zane stepped through the door and into the shop. I made sure to lock up behind him. I didn't want any interruptions. I tried to slow my racing heart as we walked hand in hand up the staircase to my apartment. It felt weird, yet right, leading Zane up to my home.

"Homemade frozen pizza and cherry wine? You're my kind of girl," he teased, handing me a bouquet of freshly picked flowers.

Arranging them in a vase, I threw some sarcasm right back at him. "And a bouquet, freshly picked from my front yard flower garden. You're my kind of guy!" I barely got the words out when he pulled me into his arms and kissed me.

"Ahem. Hate to let this gourmet meal get cold," I said.

I poured two glasses of wine and took a sip, watching his eyes. He had a strange hungry look on his face, and I'm pretty sure it wasn't for the frozen pizza I'd made for dinner.

Before I knew it, he'd downed the entire glass of wine.

"I'm no connoisseur, but this is pretty good. You wouldn't be trying to get me drunk so you can take advantage of me, would you?" he asked as I refilled his glass.

I took a small sip. My head was already feeling like a

helium-filled balloon. The last thing I wanted to do was get too drunk. I'm a total lightweight, and that would be a disaster.

"No. I'm just trying to get you to overlook my lack of culinary skills," I said, my foot accidentally brushing up against his leg. Chills swept over my body.

"This is a really nice apartment. It's much bigger than I expected it to be."

"It's definitely big enough for the three of us, although there are times when it feels pretty cramped, despite the size. Like when we're all trying to get ready to go somewhere. I have to admit, another bathroom would come in handy with three girls sharing the apartment."

"Yeah, I can see where that might be an issue."

"Would you like me to show you around?" I asked, unsure of which direction our conversation was headed.

"Absolutely."

Standing up faster than I should have, my legs felt like putty, and I wobbled slightly. I needed to slow down on the wine before my carefully planned evening turned into a total disaster thanks to my inability to hold my alcohol.

"Obviously, this is the kitchen and dining room. Down the hall are our bedrooms and the bathroom. And over there is the living room."

I grabbed his hand and tugged him behind me into the living room.

"You have to check this out." It was my favorite room in the entire apartment, and I was about to show Zane why. Our living room faced the bay and had a balcony which ran the entire length of the building.

"Wow. What an amazing view," he said, looking out over the town's lights shimmering across the dark water.

I finished the rest of my wine in one gulp and set down my glass.

So much for slowing down on the alcohol.

"I've always wondered what it would be like to be kissed by you while we were standing in this very spot," I whispered.

"Let's see if I can solve that mystery for you." He moved closer, cupping my face gently in his hands.

"I love you, Emmy."

My heart melted when I heard his sweet words. And I had to confess, I'd fallen for my demon. "I love you too."

As he kissed me, his hands slid slowly down my back, sending wave after wave of heat through my body. It never ceased to amaze me at how my body reacted to Zane's touch.

It seemed like we kissed forever, teasing one another with each swipe of our tongues. Surprisingly, he pulled back from the kiss and spun me around to face the bay. His body pressed against my back side. He brushed my hair to the side. His lips quickly found the back of my neck.

Oh God. It felt so good.

His hands slowly explored my curves, then leisurely traveled back up before brushing lightly over my breasts. I leaned my head back, enjoying every sensation humming through me and closed my eyes.

In the past, whenever his hands drifted toward any of my more personal zones, I'd gently nudged them aside, signaling that I wasn't quite ready to take the next step. But lately, I'd been letting his touch wander, roaming more freely toward those private areas.

It was time to actively encourage him. The little gasp I let out was my signal—I'd finally surrendered to his touch.

Spinning around to face Zane, I pressed my lips against his. My hands meandered across his chest and down his stomach, pausing at his waist. My desire to take things up a notch had come across loud and clear, judging by the firmness I felt in his pants when he pressed up against me. I'd brushed up against his desire once before, then hastily retreated, determined to keep my innocence intact. I had no such desire to retreat tonight.

I pulled back from the lingering kiss, and tugged Zane into the candlelit living room. We collapsed on the couch which was located quite close to the balcony doors.

His hands and mouth once again explored my neck and shoulders. Nudging the thin straps of my dress aside, the little fabric slipped, ever so slightly. Yet it was enough to reveal my breasts.

His breath hitched in his throat, as did mine. I wasn't sure if I should pull the material back up, or if I should leave it as is.

Turns out, Zane had made the decision for me when his lips brushed the top of my breast, then closed over my nipple, sucking it gently into his mouth.

I wanted to scream all the naughty words building in my mind, but the words thankfully stayed trapped in my head.

Oh my God! What have I been missing!

Every new kiss—every new touch felt amazing, but I couldn't let this be all about me. I wanted to be an active participant. So, turnabout being fair play and all, I leaned back and pushed him away before stripping off his t-shirt. The sight of Zane shirtless made my mouth water, especially the way his toned body glowed in the candlelight.

We kissed again. This time, our bare chests pressed against each other.

I never once imagined that skin on skin contact could feel so heavenly. Yeah, I know—I know, but there really was no other way to describe it. It truly was the epitome of perfection...therefore heavenly.

Zane's hands, once again, slid over my thighs, lifting the short hem of my dress until he stroked my most secret place over the silky fabric of my panties.

How it happened, I don't exactly know. It was like I was

in some sort of erotic fog. But somehow, he managed to slip off my panties and toss them over his shoulder. His touch drove me mad.

I was wild with lust and grabbed at his belt buckle.

I wanted him. All of him.

"You are so beautiful—so hot. I've wanted you since the moment we met," he whispered.

He stood up, leaving me panting. I watched as he stripped off his remaining clothes, tossing one article at a time over his shoulder.

I thought seeing someone of the opposite sex get naked in front of me would be awkward, but it wasn't. It was exciting. Besides being filled with anticipation about what was to come, I was wide-eyed and curious, and more than ready to explore every inch of Zane's body—now that it was on full display.

Am I supposed to say something? I wondered.

Did local customs dictate that I utter some dirty invitation? Everything that I'd learned from the Dark Beasts books indicated an invitation was proper sexual etiquette. The woman always begged for her lover to come to her and take her. The more Zane stood there and stared at me, the more I came to believe that some sort of sexual etiquette was needed.

I had a brief recollection of something my mother once told me. "When making conversation, compliments are always welcome."

I also remembered a magazine article which said men were inherently self-conscious about their genitalia, and you could easily give them a confidence boost with a little praise. Judging from Zane's rather large erection aimed at me like a Saturn rocket, none of that seemed at all necessary.

"Well, when in Rome..." I mumbled, quietly.

"What's that?" he asked.

Ignoring him, I summoned up my deepest, sexiest voice. I even squinted slightly to make my eyes look sexy, hoping to relay how badly I wanted him.

"Ravage me, Zane. Take my maidenhood. Thrust your throbbing, steely flesh sword—which is quite impressive, although I've nothing to compare it to, other than a few dirty pictures Chloe showed me—deep into me."

My supposed-to-be-sexy invitation flew from my mouth in one long run-on sentence that came out as more of a squeak than the husky-sexy voice I'd aimed for.

Someone, please stop me from talking.

I didn't know if I should cover my face in shame or run and hide from the embarrassment coursing through me.

Zane laughed, just a little. His eyes, needy and hungry, remained locked on my face. The embarrassment I'd felt moments ago faded as fleetingly as it had arrived. I loved how quickly he was able to turn any situation around, instantly calming my nerves.

"It's okay if you're nervous. I'd be worried if you weren't," he said, kneeling down and lifting the little black dress over my head.

I let out a gasp as I laid back on the couch and he kissed his way up my thighs.

The entire time Zane and I had been in the living room, I'd barely noticed the pedestrian chatter coming from the sidewalk below, until I heard a familiar feminine squealing along with an equally familiar cackling.

Suddenly, it sounded like a SWAT team was storming up the stairs. The familiar squeals and cackles grew progressively louder.

"Oh no! It's Jade and Chloe!" I cried, scrambling to gather up my clothes. Struggling with the flimsy little scrap of material as if I'd never dressed myself before, I clumsily tripped and fell to the floor. Rolling around like a sea lion caught in a fisherman's net, I caught a glimpse of Zane scurrying past the balcony doors, desperately searching for his discarded clothes.

My roommates flung open the apartment door and charged through the kitchen, heading right for the living room.

"Gotcha!" Chloe shouted.

"What are you doing back so soon? You were supposed to let me have the apartment for the evening. At least until midnight. We agreed on it," I growled.

"Erik and Daryl had to respond to an emergency, so we thought we'd walk to the bowling alley and hang out there for a while." She shrugged.

"Hello? Does this look like the fricking bowling alley?" I asked, pulling myself up off the floor. "You couldn't have kept walking?" I was absolutely frustrated by the turn of events.

"We would have, but a very curious thing happened that caught our attention. Just as we passed under our balcony, we spotted a silky little pair of red panties floating down from the sky." Her fingers lightly dancing in the air.

"Imagine my surprise when the panties were followed by a man's belt and a pair of boxers." Jade handed me Zane's belt. "I picked this up from the sidewalk. Your sexy red skivvies are currently dangling from the lamp post, waving like a little flag."

"And your boy's boxers are caught on the tree out front." Chloe pointed to the open balcony doors.

I rubbed my forehead. Was this really happening? Could it possibly get any worse?

"Did you finally get to...you know," she whispered.

"No. I think that ship has sailed for the night," I replied.

"Sorry, Emmy. We could've kept walking, but we weren't the only ones to notice what you and Zane were up to. We had to let you know. You've got a small drunken crowd cheering you guys on down there." Jade pointed to the balcony doors. "Hazards of living in a tourist town on a summer night. You guys can't just strip down and toss your underwear off the balcony and expect privacy."

"Oh my God," I moaned, burying my face in her shoulder. Of course, it could get worse.

Zane appeared at the balcony door wearing only his jeans.

"Oh my. Hellooo, Zane," Chloe greeted him.

"Don't worry, Emmy. I've got this." Stepping out onto the balcony, she dragged my shirtless boyfriend along like he was a mannequin.

"Show's over, everyone!" she yelled down to the mostly male group gathered below.

The little crowd of revelers laughed, accompanied by a few boos and at least two shouts of, "that was quick."

"You're just jealous of this!" She patted Zane's shoulder.

"Hey, you! Bring those panties back here!" she shouted.

Returning to the room, she looked at me apologetically. "Sorry, Emmy. Some drunken idiot shimmied up the lamppost and nabbed your underwear. Wait until that guy sobers up and realizes those are women's underwear, and he can't even wear them."

I think all of us looked at Chloe like she'd just ate a bug.

"Sorry about tonight. You guys want us to go to our rooms and you can finish doing what you were doing? Just yell when we can come back out," Jade asked.

"That's even weirder than what Chloe said," I replied.

"Thanks anyway, but I think it's time to call it a night." I handed Zane his shirt and belt.

"How about I pick you up and we'll catch breakfast, make a day of it?"

"Sounds perfect," I said, concealing my frustration, which to my surprise, wasn't fading away. I was in for a miserable, sleepless night.

CHAPTER SEVEN

$\mathcal{I}$ was awakened by the loud, familiar chatter of my friends and our neighbor, Mary. I stumbled toward the sound. I found myself instantly bewildered by the conversation I'd walked in on.

"It's important to communicate with your partner. You need to be able to tell each other what you like, what you want, what you need," Mary explained.

"Can you give us an example?" Jade asked.

"Everyone's different, I suppose. Tim and I have never been shy. As a matter of fact, we met when I was a waitress, and he was a short order cook. We were in the routine of blurting out what we needed—quick and to the point. And out of habit, I guess you could say, we developed our own lingo for everything, like 'cowgirl with spurs wheelbarrow style!' or 'sixty-nine with a hot top in the alley!'. I swear, sometimes our bedroom sounded like it was Sunday morning at the Waffle Hut."

"Did you like to role play about being at work or something?" Jade asked.

"Role play? Now that's a whole different topic," Mary

answered. "But getting back to positions, lately, we've been trying a variation I like to call kitty style."

"Kitty style? What's that?" Chloe asked.

"It's just like doggy style, except with a little biting and scratching."

"Zombie alert!" Jade shouted, announcing my arrival.

"Brains being in short supply, the zombie opted for caffeine." I narrated my trip to the tea pot. Pouring a cup, I joined them at the table.

"Good morning, Mary. What brings you here at such an early hour?"

"Tim and I heard the little crowd of tourists gathered under your balcony last night, and witnessed the panties floating down, and...well...truth be told, I was just curious as to who got laid last night. But the girls filled me in on what happened. Oh, and they told me the good news about how you destroyed the evidence from that delicate matter we'd discussed. So, I guess, that means the case is closed. Thank you so much. I knew I could count on all of you."

I watched as the tension instantly drained from Mary's face. Even if I didn't have all the answers, we still knew who had been responsible for blackmailing the women of Angel Bay, and all the evidence of his blackmailing scheme had been destroyed.

"Yeah, and now she's thanking us by giving us the sex-ed info that we never learned back home," Chloe added.

"Chloe just had to tell her that we're all still virgins." Jade rolled her eyes.

"About that. Try not to make such a big deal about it. You're all adults." Mary leaned back, preparing to offer more sage advice. "Listen, losing your virginity is like finally buying your first minivan. Yeah, it hurts a little and you might even be a little disappointed in yourself. But then you suddenly realize all the things you can actually fit in there."

Her hands animated a shoving motion, as if she was stuffing a turkey.

I spat my tea back into the mug. "Jesus!"

"No, no. What I mean is that you finally realize how convenient it is not to have the whole virginity thing being a mental block. You can be with the man you love and just be spontaneous. It's actually liberating. And like a minivan, it becomes simply practical."

"I'm pretty sure Emmy was well on her way to getting smashed by Zane's minivan when we walked in last night," Jade said.

Chloe nudged me. "What exactly was Zane about to do when we interrupted you?"

I felt the rush of blood to my face, and I tried not to laugh. "Um...Dark Beasts, book thirty-three, chapter eight."

"Ha! I knew it. Fangsgiving! That book is a real classic. I just so happen to have my copy handy," she replied.

"Oh God," I mumbled.

Clearing her throat, Chloe flipped through the worn and tattered pages of her beloved book. "Straddling him, she leaned down and grasped his huge throbbing manhood. She stroked his shaft like a cocaine-crazed monkey working a butter churn until—"

"No. Not that part. Next scene," I replied.

Chloe flipped a few more pages. "It must have been the effects of lapping up the sweet juices from her sex which awakened his wolf. Suddenly, he worked his tongue into her folds with all the fury of a starved dog trying to lick out the last remnants of peanut butter from a jar."

"Yep. I think that's what he was about to do," I said, smiling but unable to look my friends in the eye.

"Oh my. I can't say I've ever heard it put quite that way." Mary shook her head, obviously trying to shake a disturbing visual from her mind. "I don't know who writes that stuff. Oh well, I'm sure you'll be in for a real treat once you get another opportunity. In any case, I need to get home. Thanks again, ladies," she said, heading for the door.

"Now, back to Zane. You need to interrogate him. Don't let that charming demon spawn distract you again, Emmy," Jade said.

"Yeah." Chloe nodded. "I'm sure it's his plan. He's seducing you, so you'll quit trying to figure out what he is, and what else he knows about the strange case of the missing beast from the studio."

"Getting distracted is my own fault. But can you blame me? And now, I'm going crazy after last night." I closed my eyes and pictured how he stood boldly in front of me—naked, muscular and rock hard.

"See? It's already happening behind those closed eyelids of hers," Jade said.

Chloe snapped her fingers. "Hey, Emmy. At least give us some more details about what Zane was doing to you when we walked in...for paranormal research purposes, of course."

"All I'm going to say about it is, next time, we'll go to his place."

"What happened to keeping everything on your terms and your turf?" Jade asked.

"A pair of party crashers happened. That's what," I sighed.

The heavy footsteps on the stairs up to our apartment signaled Zane's arrival.

"Speak of the devil," Jade said, getting up to open the door.

"Good morning, ladies. No need to flatter me with a promotion, Jade. Are you ready for breakfast, Emmy?"

How was he so cheery? Did he not feel half of the frustration I felt? That my body felt?

"Hmm, breakfast. Is that what they call it?" Chloe teased. "Quite a menu, you have there, Zane."

I was convinced that she just couldn't seem to help herself when it came to teasing us about our failed romantic evening. It was part of the reason I loved her so darn much. Chloe could make me smile, even in the worst of moments.

"Please ignore these perverts." I didn't waste another second, greeting Zane with a hug and a kiss.

"I can't stop thinking about last night," I whispered. "Let's go to your place."

Hopeful for some extended time alone, I'd taken the time during the night to pack for a sexy overnight stay. And I did it very discreetly, jamming my things into a beach bag to avoid any more awkward teasing from my friends.

"Ah, I forgot. I promised my mom we'd stop by and have breakfast with her and my sister. But after that, the day is ours. I promise, it will be worth the wait."

Despite everything, I had to admit I was still a bit anxious. But when Zane wrapped his arms around me, I calmed instantly. He made me feel safe, and I truly trusted him.

CHAPTER EIGHT

*O*ut by the truck, Zane's golden retriever, Mooch, greeted me with a flurry of kisses. Wedging himself between me and Zane, he was determined to remain the center of attention.

I didn't mind. After all, I was infringing on his territory.

Arriving at Eve's farmhouse, I spotted two cars parked out front.

"Hey there, lovebirds," his sister said, greeting us from the porch.

"Hi, Angel. Where's Mom?"

"Inside. Taking care of...unfinished business, apparently," she replied, buffing a file across her nails.

"Are we early?" I asked.

"Nope. She's just running late, as usual."

As soon as Zane and I walked through the front door, I heard Eve engaged in a conversation. Wrapping his fingers around mine, we headed for the kitchen.

Just as we turned the corner, I froze in my tracks. Seated at the kitchen table was Ash. Yes, the handsome mysterious stranger who had showed up at our store during a sudden storm. Though, today, he looked a bit different. He had apparently swapped his perfectly tailored suit for a bathrobe.

He turned to face me and smiled. "Emmy. What a pleasant surprise seeing you here."

I was truly at a loss for words.

"What?" I asked.

But it wasn't directed toward Ash. Instead, I had turned and spoken to Zane. And somewhere in the back of my mind was Chloe professing her vampiric suspicions about Ash.

"You've met?" Zane asked. A confused look crossed his handsome face.

"We certainly have. A while back I blew into town and stopped by Midge's shop, only to find the proprietorship had changed to the beautiful and capable hands of Miss Emerald and her lovely associates. I do say, son, you have excellent taste. I only introduced myself as Ash. I didn't realize the two of you were friends or I would have spent a little more time introducing myself and getting to know Emerald."

"Son?" I asked. "You're his—"

"Emmy, this is my father, Duke Ashtaroth of Hell."

Eve, wrapped in a long silky robe, stepped into the kitchen.

"Zane, you're early," she said, pouring two cups of coffee and handing one to Ash.

"Ah, Eve, your coffee reflects your personality, dark and bitter," Ash said.

"And too hot for you," she replied.

Tapping his thigh, he invited her to sit on his lap. "I didn't hear any complaints last night. Or this morning."

Blowing the steam off her cup, Eve accepted Ash's invitation and sat on his lap. "What can I say, sometimes I'm known to be charitable to the needy. And I've also been known to cook breakfast for men I should've poisoned."

"Okay, enough. We're right here," Zane said.

Lifting the teaspoon from her cup, she softly waved it like it was a magic wand. "Fine. I did promise breakfast," she replied.

Bowls, utensils, and ingredients magically levitated. Suddenly, the objects swirled about in a wild flurry. I felt my mouth involuntarily drop open as I witnessed Eve's culinary magic in action.

Noticing my amazement, she smiled. "Handy, isn't it? Are you ready to come to the dark side, Emmy? I'd love to convert an angel."

Ash cocked his head, amused and very curious. "Emmy's an angel? Interesting. Are you sure? I think I would have sensed it if it were true."

"Mom! You promised to keep that between us," Zane growled.

Raising my hand, I attempted to politely diffuse the issue. "Practically an angel. And it's fine, Zane. After all, you are all family."

"She's exactly right," Ash said, nodding to Zane. "I'm liking her more by the minute."

"As far as I can tell, she's somehow cloaked her true nature. Isn't that right, Emmy?" Eve said, continuing to command her kitchen with a teaspoon.

I couldn't lie, but I definitely worried about dishing out too much private information. "Something like that," I said.

"First, I find out Midge's shop has been overrun by angels, then I find out my son snagged the prettiest one for himself. I really need to stop in more often."

"What brings you by this time?" Zane asked.

"Last time I came through town, I was looking for Dexter —who is still missing by the way. But now something else of mine has gone missing, the Heart of the Phoenix."

Angel stepped into the room. "How interesting. Need any

help, Mom?" she asked, pulling a wand from her back pocket. Yes, an honest-to-goodness witch's wand.

"Set the table, dear," Eve directed.

Sweeping the wand in front of her, she appeared to trace out letters with the tip. Sure enough, the cupboard doors flung open, and dishes floated onto the table to create the perfect place settings.

Being a natural born sleuth, I was intrigued by the missing Dexter and the Heart of the Phoenix. I listened carefully to the conversations and avoided bringing up the topics directly.

Although the missing subjects never came up, I was able to learn more about Zane's dad.

"How have our Hellions been getting along?" he asked Eve.

I thought the way he referred to them as "our Hellions" was interesting. I'd previously assumed Eve was the sole guardian of the Hellions, as if they were her personal creatures. But instead, tending to the Hellions was, in fact, a joint venture between Eve and Ash.

I also deduced that Ash would have to be a demon of a higher rank or class than the lowly Hellions. As far as his relationship with Eve, it was best summed up by a comment Angel made.

"So, Dad, you think you and Mom can schedule your next booty call for Labor Day weekend? My band is playing a gig for the town's End of Summer Bash."

"Don't worry. If he gives an excuse, I'll just summon him back to Angel Bay."

Eve's response was telling. It was clear she held considerable influence over Ash, which certainly meant they still maintained a sort of relationship—an arrangement which seemed complicated and completely foreign to me. Were they a couple who had split up? Were they now just part-time lovers? I'd never met anyone like them.

You see, the couples in Heaven were happy—not just happyish. Their relationships were perfect—as in zero arguments or quarrels between spouses. There was never any jealousy or hurt feelings, therefore, there was nothing to be upset about. A couple who might have fought over money problems while living, had all they needed in Heaven. Problem solved. As far as I knew, I was the only unhappy soul in Heaven.

This banter, the sexual tension between them, was fascinatingly new to me. They clearly cared deeply for each other, despite whatever problems they had in their past.

I also learned Angel was in a band. It was news to me, but not as big as the news that she was also a witch—a quite accomplished witch to boot. It was obvious Eve had a great influence on her.

As far as Ash goes, I wasn't sure. Her attitude toward him was lukewarm, lightly sprinkled with just a dash of spite and a hint of resentment. Even still, he was her dad, and it was especially important for him to be present for the concert to see her performance.

But there was no more mention of Dexter nor the Heart of the Phoenix. I was happily surprised the conversation was light and pleasant, and I wasn't the target of an inquisition. That isn't to say Zane and I, as a couple, didn't find ourselves the target of the supernatural family.

It was Eve who zeroed in first. "You know, Zane's cabin is just a mile up the road and there's plenty of privacy."

Her statement caught me by surprise, and I worried she somehow was all too aware of our plans for the day. It wouldn't have shocked me in the least if telepath was listed on her supernatural resume.

Zane started to choke on his pancake.

"Uh—yeah, I suppose so." I shrugged and stammered, unable to make eye contact.

"I'm just saying that it would be a nice cozy home for a

young couple to start off their lives together," she said.

Zane managed to choke down his food. "Mom. We're... you're making all these assumptions already about me and Emmy. I mean, come on, we're just..."

I felt, or maybe even heard, some annoying twang in my head—like a single banjo string being plucked.

"We're just what?" I blurted out.

Zane gulped. "We're just, you know, getting started with our relationship. We haven't even talked about those sorts of things."

"Good answer, big brother. I thought you were about to perform a total faceplant with a 'we're just friends' comment," Angel added.

"Agreed," I replied, my weak voice betraying my own concerns. I did, however, elicit a chuckle from both Eve and Ash.

On our way back to the truck, Zane flipped open his pocketknife and cut a bright bouquet from Eve's flower beds.

"Maybe I can find something to put those in at my place. Sorry I haven't invited you over before, but my spartan little hut isn't much compared to your comfortable apartment."

"I'm happy to be wherever you are," I said, taking in the sweet floral fragrance of the bouquet. "As long as it has indoor plumbing," I teased, but I was dead serious.

"It even has electricity. When the wind blows."

I really hoped he was joking.

Mooch relinquished the center position on the bench seat, allowing me to cozy up next to Zane.

This is it. Finally. For sure. The big moment. We're going over to his house, with one goal in mind.

My realization eclipsed any curiosity I had about Ash, Dexter, the Heart of the Phoenix, or the dynamics of Zane's family relationships.

CHAPTER NINE

*T*he road to his cabin reminded me of a gravel snake crafting a path through ancient pines, and it made me feel like we'd not only traveled in distance but back in time as well. We seemed a world away from Angel Bay, or even Eve's farmhouse.

Bouncing and squeaking into a clearing, we came to a stop, and I got my first look at Zane's cabin. It was more rustic than I hoped, but certainly not the dilapidated shack he made it out to be. It was an atypical log cabin with a field stone chimney, and a large, covered porch. An old-time windmill stood next to a building which looked like a large shed or a garage. Completing the quaint log cabin scene was a small brook that bubbled through the grassy meadow.

"It looks so peaceful and cozy back here, it's like we traveled into a painting. Amazing. This isn't one of your mystical portals, is it?"

"A magic portal? Emmy, who needs magic when I'm here to deliver your every fantasy."

I appreciated his lighthearted display of confidence; it calmed my excited heart.

"Wow, every fantasy? Am I a lucky angel or what?"

Mooch announced our arrival with a single bark. Leaping through the window, he disappeared in a patch of tall grass.

Zane held my hand, steadying me as I stepped down from the running board.

"My mansion awaits."

Strolling up the path to the cabin, I got a closer look at the aged lumber. I could tell the cabin was ancient and certainly had a long history.

"If this place could talk, I bet it would have some interesting stories to tell."

"Hey, I know I have a reputation, but it's not as legendary as people make it out to be. It's mostly exaggerated."

"Uh, I meant that your cabin is really old. I bet it has some cool history," I replied, a bit startled by his response.

"But as long as we're on the topic, what do you mean by 'mostly exaggerated'? Not quite as many notches on your bedpost as rumor has it?"

Cocking my head, I waited for his response. I felt weird, like I was half amused, and half perturbed, as if I was jealous or something. The latter being completely unreasonable for me to feel that way. And it bothered me that I did.

"I'm not sure what the rumors say, exactly. But whatever they are, don't believe them. Especially if they're coming from my mom. She thinks I've been with every girl in the county."

"Every girl? Impressive."

"Yeah, she's way off. I'm only halfway through the list," he said, opening the front door.

"And welcome to my home."

I had deliberately kept my expectations for his cabin on the low side. Which, in retrospect, turned out to be a good plan because I have to admit, I was doubly impressed when I saw it was not only neat and clean, but actually quite cozy and inviting. The main room was a large living room on one side, and a smaller kitchen area which was separated by a long countertop. It reminded me of the sort of setup I'd see at a diner.

Assorted antique tools hung on the log walls—which I was relieved to see. God knows how I would've reacted if Zane had stuffed animal heads on display instead.

The far wall was nothing more than a massive fireplace, which appeared to be the only source of heat. I had yet to experience a winter in Angel Bay, but I was certain the fireplace would heat every inch of Zane's cabin and then some.

His furniture consisted of an overstuffed couch and chair, both pretty old, but amazingly comfortable looking. They faced a giant wooden coffee table. Judging from the various parts and screws strewn haphazardly across the surface, it apparently doubled as a motorcycle engine workbench.

A small TV, which looked like it hadn't been watched in decades, sat on a little table in the corner.

"Just a warning, Mooch prefers this end of the couch." Zane slapped the cushion. "And he's not used to sharing it."

"Noted." I could easily see Mooch passed out on his corner of the couch while Zane tinkered with an engine.

"Back there is the bathroom, beyond that, there are a couple of closets and my bedroom," he said, and quickly steered the conversation away from our unspoken hopes for later.

"We have a cold front heading our way. There are a few storms nearby, but the forecast says they shouldn't be here until much later. As long as the weather holds, I was wondering if you'd like to go for a walk on one of the trails? I see you brought your beach bag. Maybe we could even stop by the glen again and go for a swim."

"Sure. That sounds like fun."

Even Zane had assumed my beach bag was filled with— well, beach stuff.

Sneaking a peek at his bedroom, I was able to catch a glimpse of his queen size poster bed and a single matching end table. I know it was dumb of me, but I squinted in an attempt to see if the bed posts had notches—as if he'd actually carved a bizarre erotic totem pole to display a record of his conquests.

"Maybe later, I can grill up some food and we can relax by the firepit out back?"

"That sounds even better."

I was happy when he didn't make any assumptions for our evening activities. That is, whether I was going to spend the night with him. Although, it was something I desperately wanted to happen, but only if that course developed naturally.

"Great. Let me grab something out of the freezer so it has time to defrost."

I heard him rustling around in the kitchen while I took a closer look at the framed photographs hanging in the hallway. Some were of him and his sister, some included Eve, and only a couple of them included Ash, who appeared only in the older photographs. It was interesting and a little fun to catch a glimpse into Zane's life, but it stirred up my natural curiosity. I wanted to learn more about their family history.

An additional set of vintage black and white photographs also hung on the wall. Those portraits depicted a couple in vintage clothes. "Ash and Eve? They haven't aged a day. How?" I whispered. The pictures sure looked like antiques, but I convinced myself they were novelty portraits you can have taken by a photographer at a local fair.

"Ready?" Zane asked.

Mooch barked, apparently answering for me.

From the meadow behind the house, the trail led us into a

shadowy world of tall pines and huge ferns. Perhaps it's why my thoughts turned to the more somber events of the previous week, and I felt it was a good time to bring them up.

"Did you know Mike Schmitz?"

"The guy with the old photography studio, right? I've seen him around, but I don't know him."

"He passed away the other evening."

"Really? That's too bad. What happened?"

"Apparently, he had a heart attack. He dropped dead right in front of his studio."

Zane's question was a perfectly normal response to the news. Anyone would react that way.

Anyone except Kathy.

When I broke the news to her, the response was quite different.

She wasn't even a little bit curious about how Mike Schmitz died. There was no "Oh my God! How did it happen?" Nope. She had taken for granted that he must have been ill. It was very weird.

I filled Zane in on the mysterious extortion cases we'd been working on. The only thing I left out was Chloe's vampire suspicions. Now that I knew for certain Ash was not a vampire, I figured it would be silly to even mention it.

"He could have been using hypnosis or even some sort of drugs. He definitely used something to control them," Zane said, stopping dead in his tracks.

"There had to be more of a motive than blackmailing them for money. There are any number of ways he could have illegally obtained the cash he wanted or needed. My best guess was that he targeted those women with the goal of humiliating them."

"Good point. The downside of being a naïve angel is that I'll never understand the depraved motives of some individuals. The people in Heaven are pure. They just don't do things like that."

I was beginning to think we were in way over our heads. How could we ever understand what drove these people to do such awful things?

"Anyway, we had planned on going back the next morning to scope the place out, but when we got there, we noticed Mike's studio door was open. So, we searched the place like we'd originally planned. We found evidence—piles of cash, compromising photos of his victims—it all proved that he was the one blackmailing the women. But we didn't find any proof of how he did it. We did find an empty cage, though. That was really odd."

I still worried about whatever had made those claw marks. What happened to it? Where did it go?

"A cage? What kind of cage? That's an odd thing to find in a photography studio."

The look on Zane's face went from concerned to straight up worried.

"Emmy, how big was the cage you found?"

"Big. I should have called it a jail cell rather than a cage. It had iron bars, the works. Whatever was in there clawed the heck out of the walls. It either broke out on its own or someone helped it. Either way, it wasn't just released. Plus, the deadbolt on the front door of Mike's studio was melted. I bet we're dealing with a felonious metal worker armed with a blow torch—a true villain. Only, he or she wasn't interested in the cash Mike Schmitz had. Instead, the goal was to release a caged—?" I was about to say monster but stopped short. I had no idea what was in that cage. A light flickered in my head... what if it was one of the Hellions who had been locked up by Mike?

Mooch barked, dancing around us. Even he knew something was amiss.

It was the forecast, as usual, which proved to be wrong. A strong gust of wind and a crack of thunder rolled through the whispering pines. They began to bend and bow with the force of the squall. All around, we heard the eerie creaks and cracks of branches twisting and snapping.

"We need to head back to the house," Zane said. Now he was alarmed.

"You know what it is, don't you?"

"Maybe. But right now, the weather has me more worried."

Before I knew it, we'd reversed our course and were running through a torrential downpour. By the time we raced through the open meadow and made it into the cabin, we were soaked to our skin. Mooch shook himself, showering me mercilessly while I shrieked and laughed. I was already drenched. A little more water wasn't going to hurt.

Zane grabbed a stack of towels from the linen closet just as the power went out. Lighting a kerosene lantern and a few candles, he made his way over to the fireplace.

"I'll get this started so we can warm up. Do you have any dry clothes in your bag to change into?"

I grabbed a candle so I could navigate through the complete darkness that filled Zane's cabin. I snatched my beach bag off the couch and headed for the bathroom.

"As a matter of fact, I do. I'll be right back."

I stripped down and hung my soaked clothes over the tub to dry. I wrapped myself in a towel and pawed around in my bag, looking for something to change into. I set aside the super skimpy, sexy, see-through negligée which I brought along just in case the opportunity arose. There were other odds and ends which I thought to grab, but not a single pair of pants or a dry shirt.

"Dang it. Well, that leaves only this." I held up the ridiculous negligée I'd packed.

Donning the transparent material, I shivered. "What was I thinking?"

I couldn't stroll out there dressed in this. It covered absolutely nothing.

Geez.

He was going to think I was some sort of desperate hussy. Peaking in the linen closet, I found a plush gray blanket and wrapped myself in it. Returning to the living room, Zane had a fire roaring and was warming himself beside it.

"You look cozy. It's my turn to get out of these wet clothes. The fire is nice and warm. You should go stand by it for a few minutes to chase away the chills."

I laughed. If he only knew how uncomfortable I felt wearing my ridiculous outfit. When I was sure he'd left the room, I opened the blanket and let the waves of heat soak through me.

Mooch stared, panted, and stared some more.

"Would you mind? I could use a little privacy."

Rolling onto his back and closing his eyes, it was clear he'd understood my request.

The wind howled relentlessly, and rain pelted the windows. It seemed to be nearly dark outside. Altogether, the storm made the fire feel all the cozier. Zane returned, wearing a bathrobe and bearing two steaming mugs of tea.

I wrapped my blanket firmly around my body and took a seat next to him on the couch. I sipped slowly at my hot tea.

"When we were out on the trail, you seemed alarmed when I mentioned the empty cage. What do you think was in there?"

"I can't be sure," he said, blowing the steam from his mug. "This morning at breakfast, do you remember the conversation where my dad mentioned that he was looking for Dexter?"

"Sure do. I was really curious. But I didn't want to come off as being nosey, so I didn't ask him."

"Dexter is my dad's...dog. Well, technically, he's a hellhound. He looks like a giant mastiff, but he's much larger than any dog you would've ever seen. Most of the time, he's super friendly and helpful. Hellhounds have a variety of powers, one of them being mind control. Dexter is always eager to please. Mostly."

"Oh my god! So Mike Schmitz somehow learned about this and got control of Dexter to do his bidding. That's probably what he kept in that cage."

"That's my guess, but it begs the question. How did he ever learn about hellhounds, and Dexter in particular?"

"Those are good questions. You said Dexter is eager to please, 'mostly'. What did you mean by that?"

"In order for hellhounds to be trained—docile and all—they need to fulfill their guarding instincts. Long ago, Dad gave Dexter a necklace to guard. Not just any necklace, but one called the Heart of the Phoenix. Like I said, Dexter is nothing but an overgrown puppy...until someone takes away the one thing he has been given to guard. Then he turns into a pure hellhound."

My eyes nearly popped out of my head, my voice quivering. "Hellhound?"

Images of the huge claw marks and twisted metal bars in the studio flashed through my mind. It all made sense. The reason the women couldn't remember having those pictures taken, the cage, the claw marks.

"That does not sound good."

"When Dexter is in his hellhound state, he's unpredictable at best," he said, shifting his gaze to the rain battered windows.

Pulling me against him, he whispered, "But I don't think

we have anything to worry about, if that's what you're wondering."

Zane's sexy voice and strong arms proved to be the perfect distraction, and forced me to push aside any fears of the raging storm or Dexter the runaway hellhound.

Normally for me, this was the cue for the weird part of my brain to kick in. It's what gives me that amazing ability to change any perfect moment into a cringingly awkward train wreck. To preempt myself from blurting out something totally embarrassing, I kissed him.

Zane's hand slid under the blanket. He cocked his head to the side as his fingers brushed against my negligée.

"Hmmm. What do we have here?"

He pulled the blanket back, his jaw dropped. The hunger I'd noticed in his eyes last night had returned. Suddenly, I didn't feel so silly about packing my negligée.

"You look like an angel."

"Practically an angel." I pulled him closer for a kiss.

I leaned back to let his kiss wander from my mouth to my neck, reveling in each new sensation sweeping through my body.

I untied his robe and pushed it off his shoulders. Bathed in the flickering glow of the fire, his naked body seemed like a perfect sculpture which had magically been brought to life.

Trailing my fingertips over his broad chest and down his muscular torso, I began to pant like a puppy.

I whispered, "My hands traveled over the hard landscape of his washboard abs and danced slowly around the base of his hard, throbbing manhood. Wrapping it with both hands, as if she was holding a mighty erotic python, she marveled at the glorious wonder in her hands."

Lightly stroking him, my voice quivered. "I'm doing it again. Aren't I?"

"Umm, it's fine by me."

"No, I mean narrating everything out loud, like I'm in one of my steamy stories. It's just that I'm a little nervous. I don't know what to do and...and I've never touched anyone like this."

"Well, I think it's kinda cute. I also think we should pick up where we left off last night."

He slid from the couch and knelt in front of me. Parting my thighs with his kisses and his hands, he moved closer to his goal.

It was at that point, I experienced something much better than anything described in the Dark Beasts stories.

Running my fingers through his hair, my body tensed and shook repeatedly. I never imagined such a feeling could be possible. I'd read about the deed, but having never experienced it until now...

Wow!

Just after Zane had brought me to my first climax, we heard a long, lonely howl rising above the din, created by the storm ravaging the forest.

Zane paused, just for a second, to listen. When he resumed his carnal kisses, he swiftly brought me to dizzying new heights.

His mouth, his hands, and his fingers grew hotter with each touch.

Like a woman possessed, I heard my own voice uttering profane words which had never before passed my lips.

I urged him, begged him, praised him.

At that moment, I knew what he was.

Truthfully, I'd known it all along.

As I continued to cradle his head with my hands, I felt them—a short pair of horns had magically erupted. They were barely concealed by his thick hair. I wasn't shocked. I wasn't disturbed or disgusted.

Instead, I gripped his horns tight and pulled his head into

me. Encouraged by my acceptance, his tongue became longer and more agile. Instantly taken to a new orgasmic plane, everything became a blur.

I was barely aware that he had lifted me up and was carrying me toward the bedroom. The tips of his shiny black horns barely protruded from his dark hair. His eyes glowed.

I swear they emitted a pale blue light which entranced me.

"You're not frightened?"

"Excuse the pun, but it turns me on how horny you are."

Once he placed me on the bed, all sense of time was lost. I surprised myself by reciprocating his sensual kisses. Marveled by his size, shape, and—dare I say it—his taste, it was as if I was on my knees worshipping him.

Without needing a second to recover, he laid me back on the pillows and gently guided himself into me.

Our magical afternoon turned into a magical night. Somehow, over the course of our passionate adventures, we ended up back in the living room, sprawled out on a pile of blankets in front of the fire, spent of energy.

Even Zane's horns had retracted.

The howling resumed, and I noticed how closely Zane paid attention to it. Even Mooch cocked his head, curious to the sound.

"Wolves?" I asked.

"No, not around here. Natural wolves steer clear of this area. More than likely, it's the Hellions. Whenever there's a bad storm, they take to the forest. It's like one big, wild party for them."

"What do you mean by 'more than likely'. You seem to think it could be something else."

"It could be Dexter. It's not likely, though. Still, it's worth keeping an eye and ear out."

"Hmm." I traced my finger down his torso.

"Sorry about the language I used tonight. I don't know what got into me. Should I feel ashamed?"

"Oh, I know what got into you. And no, you shouldn't feel ashamed."

Quietly running my hands over his naked body, I watched him harden in the firelight. The tips of his horns reappeared through his hair.

"Good. Then make me talk dirty to you again," I whispered.

CHAPTER TEN

*Z*ane's truck squeaked to a stop. It took some nudging to get past Mooch, but I was able to squeeze in a goodbye kiss.

"I had the most perfect weekend. I don't know what you did to me, but all I can think about is you doing it again. Everything," I whispered.

"I feel the same. Maybe I can come up with something even more romantic next weekend. Tonight, I'll be helping my dad track down Dexter."

Shifting his gaze past me, he nodded. "Good luck with the inquisition."

"Ugh." I groaned, turning around to see my friends conferring on the porch like a pair of detectives preparing for an interrogation.

As I made my way up the walkway, Chloe was the first to greet me. "It's Sunday evening. By my calculations, you've been gone thirty-four hours and twenty-two minutes."

"We've got some news to share, but first, we expect the full play-by-play account of what you and Zane did. Every slutty detail," Jade added.

Settling into a wicker chair, I relented. I mean, what was the point of holding back? It would only prolong their badgering, and I was too exhausted for that.

I recalled every detail, from breakfast with Zane's family, the disclosure about Ash being Zane's dad and Angel being a witch just like Eve.

I covered the mystery of Dexter—the missing hellhound —and the little bit I knew about the Heart of the Phoenix. And lastly, I went over every single naughty act, quite explicitly. After all, if they were to ask for specifics, I couldn't lie. But there was one detail I omitted—Zane's retractable horns.

It's one thing to confess to your best friends that you were the recipient of your boyfriend's oral artistry, that you successfully reciprocated, lost your virginity, then went on to assume more positions than a crooked politician—but it's a whole other thing for an angel to confess she spent the weekend getting perfectly shagged by a horny demon.

"Now that I've confessed, what is the news you promised?" I asked.

"The missing monster is on the prowl in Angel Bay," Chloe said.

Jade jumped in, adding, "Yeah. Delbert's Used Cars and the Dairy Fairy were both nearly destroyed overnight. Everyone is talking about it. And now that we know about Dexter, he must be the culprit."

"Couldn't the damage have been from the storm?" I asked.

"He chewed the tires off a pickup truck, and chewed up the ice cream cone sculpture like it was a giant dog toy," Chloe replied. "We have to help catch that hellhound before he kills someone."

"You're right. And assuming it was Dexter who'd been caged in Mike's studio, it proves there must be a way to capture him," I said, pondering our next move—or if we even needed to worry about it. "In any case, Zane and his dad are already on the hunt for Dexter." I yawned. "I'm sure they know what they're doing."

"How does one capture a hellhound anyway?" Jade asked. "Didn't you and Zane discuss all this?"

"Not really. We had other things in mind. And now, I'm exhausted," I said, and staggered upstairs to my bed.

"You know it's our mission to look after this town and the people who live here!" Chloe shouted.

"In the morning," I groaned.

She was right, but I convinced myself that Zane and his dad would take care of it. I was certain we would just be in their way.

Until it was actually the morning.

Frantic pounding on the storefront door woke me up. Outside, the sky was beginning to take on a faint pink hue.

"The sun's not even up yet," I groaned.

Worried and listening carefully, I heard a female voice desperately shouting my name. Wrapping myself in a robe, I joined Chloe and Jade, who'd also been roused by our visitor.

Jade bumped into Chloe and the pair wobbled down the hallway like gyrating tops that were quickly running out of spin.

"How badly can you screw up that you need to buy a gift this early in the morning?" Chloe asked.

Jade shoved Chloe out of her way. "No. I bet Zane has a pissed off ex, and she's out on our front porch, ax in hand, waiting for Emmy. Maybe we should just sacrifice her so we can go back to sleep."

"Thanks a lot," I mumbled.

"Emmy! Emmy! It's Angel! I need your help!"

"Zane's sister!" Now, I was worried. Something terrible had happened, I was certain. I'd rather face the wrath of a crazed, ax-slinging ex than to learn tragic news.

The three of us rushed downstairs and ushered Angel into the store. "Wha—what's wrong?" I could barely speak.

"Mom, Dad, and Zane. They're all missing. I—I've been looking everywhere. I don't know who else to turn to. Please help," she stammered, collapsing into my arms.

"Of course," I said, trying to keep my own emotions together.

"Just try to explain, calmly, what happened."

"They went into the woods, back behind Zane's cabin. Right around sunset. Looking for Dexter. They haven't come home yet, Emmy. And it's all my fault."

"Here," Jade said, handing Angel a glass. "Drink this."

She sniffed it and gave Jade a skeptical side-eyed glance. "What's in it?"

"Various herbal extracts, a bit of angelic magic, and brandy. Mostly brandy. It's one of our anxiety cures. Go on, it'll calm your nerves."

Angel downed it like it was a shot of tequila. Twisting her face and turning her neck, she let out a squeak. "Judas priest! That was nasty."

But thirty seconds later, her breathing slowed, and she seemed to have calmed down. Her eyes looked like big, shiny black saucers, but at least she was relaxed.

"Before we just rush out into the woods looking for them, we need a lot more information. You said this was your fault. What did you mean?" Chloe asked.

Angel sucked in a deep breath and exhaled just as loud.

It seemed like she was on the brink of confessing her worst sin. She just needed a little more encouragement.

"It's okay, Angel. Whatever it is, we're on your side. We want to help. Just start at the very beginning."

"Okay, I'll try my best. Earlier this summer, Dad started showing up more often than usual. Way more often. It was nice. But I knew the real reason why he came around more often. It was because he'd been here searching for Dexter."

"Ouch," Chloe said.

"It gets worse. It's my fault because I planned it. I went through a portal and I stole the Heart of the Phoenix from Dexter's lair. When Dexter realized I had it, he followed me through the portal and back to Angel Bay."

"Well, that explains how Dexter and the Heart of the Phoenix went missing," I said. "You were behind all of it."

"Yeah. Even though I engineered the entire basis for Dad's search, it seemed like Dad's more frequent visits were actually bringing us all together. Plus, I hoped that maybe him and Mom could work things out. It seemed like we were all getting close again. I really liked it. So, in that respect, my plan was working."

"Funny, Zane never mentioned anything about your parents," I said.

"Well, Zane lives at his own place. He's always working construction jobs out of town and well...he's been a little more than distracted with you. As a matter of fact, I've barely seen him all summer. Anyway, just to be clear, our parents were never married or anything like that. They've always had their separate lives. Friends and lovers. Nothing more. But suddenly, this summer, it seemed like a romance was starting to sprout between them. A real, true love."

"I get it, Angel. You really wanted everyone to be happy," I said.

"The road to Hell is paved with good intentions," Angel sighed. "Or so they say. The trouble started almost immediately when I lost track of Dexter. I knew I had to lure him back through the portal, so I used the Heart of the Phoenix as bait. So far, he hasn't found it. And I never did track him down. I wondered if he was using his powers to conceal his location."

"Powers?" I asked.

"Hellhounds have special gifts. Besides being large and strong, they have the powers of telepathy and telekinesis."

"Mind control!" I blurted out.

"So that's how old Mike Schmitz took advantage of his victims. It wasn't hypnosis or drugs after all," Jade added.

"Mike Schmitz? The photographer who died? What does he have to do with Dexter?" Angel asked.

"We found evidence that a large beast had been imprisoned in his studio. It must have been Dexter. And I'm guessing Mike Schmitz must have been somehow using the hellhound's mind control properties to carry out an elaborate blackmail scheme. But I hate to break it to you, the beast broke out of that studio. He's not there anymore."

"Hold on," Angel said. "A large beast? I suppose it could have been Dexter. But controlling Dexter's powers to run a blackmail scheme? Theoretically, it might work. But in reality? No way. You can't just command a hellhound to do your bidding."

"There's no way at all?" I asked.

"Well, there is an old legend that says hellhounds can be summoned and forced to do your bidding. But only if you know the proper spell. It's not as easy as it sounds. Most witches will tell you straight up that spell is just a myth. Or if that spell ever truly existed, it's been lost to the world for centuries."

"Sounds like Dexter could possibly be a very valuable asset, if you had that spell," Jade said.

"Where would one look for that spell, if they thought it was real?" I asked.

Angel shrugged. "Like any spell, you'd find it in a grimoire. It'd be my first guess. Anyway, I think we're getting sidetracked. How does this help find my family?"

Thoughts and ideas were clicking in my brain, and I realized that I had started pacing around the room.

"Let's say Mike Schmitz, against all odds, managed to find that spell. And that he successfully conjured up Dexter and forced him to play a key role in extorting his victims. Then, out of pure coincidence, Mike Schmitz drops dead—on the very same day Dexter breaks loose from his prison."

"Some coincidence," Chloe said.

"Right. It's almost too convenient." I wagged my finger like it was a laser pointer. "Like Jade said, Dexter would be quite valuable. Let's just say, for argument's sake, that Mike's death wasn't natural. Maybe it was a murder. The motive? To steal Dexter and use his mind-control powers. To compound matters, Ash, Eve, and Zane go looking for Dexter and mysteriously go missing. Something smells fishy."

"That could be the old tuna sandwich I threw in the trash can yesterday," Chloe said.

Angel stared at me, wide-eyed, with the realization that I was on to something. "So, you think Mom, Dad, and Zane got too close to finding out who took Dexter, and that same person is holding them against their will?"

"It's a working theory," I said.

"But honestly, who would be able to capture a powerful witch, a Duke from Hell, and a demon? It would be nearly impossible."

"Whoa! Are you saying Zane is a demon-demon? I thought he was only part demon," Chloe yelped.

"He may only be part demon, but he still exhibits all the traits of a male demon. I'm sure Emmy knows," Angel said, shooting me a knowing glance. "After all, she spent the night with him. She must have noticed his...horns."

"Horns?" Jade nearly shouted.

"Yeah. Male demons, when they...you know...they." For

Angel, this was an awkward topic for sure. And I knew she was about to inadvertently bust me for holding back.

Chloe squinted, leaning close. "They what?"

Angel rolled her eyes. "When male demons get an erection...their horns pop out. It's a purely sexual response. Now, let's drop the subject please. It's disgusting to think of my brother's horns popping out."

Chloe and Jade were beside themselves with laughter. "Oh my gosh. You had sex with a horny devil!" Chloe teased.

Jade formed horns on her head with curved fingers. "From what you told us about the rest of his anatomy, he must've had a huge set of horns!"

"Eww, gross! Please just stop," Angel begged.

"I agree," I said, relieved to get off the topic. "Back to your point about someone being powerful enough to control your family...this is your area of expertise, Angel. We hardly know anything about demons and witches. So, if you say it's impossible, then—"

"No, I said it was *nearly* impossible. My mom always says to never rule out anything when it comes to magic."

"If we can find Dexter, we can find Zane and your parents. It's turning into a complicated case, though. Here's my suggestion for our first steps. Chloe and Jade, you both try to find out what exactly happened to Mike Schmitz. Angel and I will try to figure out if, and how, he was able to summon Dexter. If we can solve that part of the mystery, we can locate Dexter, and hopefully Zane, Ash, and Eve will be with him. Once we have those answers, we can move forward. What do you say?"

Chloe nodded. "We'll quiz Daryl and Erik for any updates. By now, the coroner should be done slicing and dicing Mike."

"That's not what it's called," Jade said.

Chloe nudged her. "Whatever. How about 'cracking open a cold one.' Seems accurate to me."

Jade groaned out a whale-like sound. "Autopsy, Chloe. It's called an autopsy."

Angel smiled. "I'm starting to think Chloe would make a better witch than an angel."

With Jade and Chloe out of the shop, it gave me the opportunity to talk to Angel some more about the topic of demons without their heckling.

A part of me wanted to learn all about Zane's secret demon identity, but I couldn't go there. As much as I wanted to, it wouldn't be fair to him. Going to his sister for information seemed way too sneaky and wrong.

But I did have pertinent questions about the demonic subject. We took a seat at the worktable in the store's backroom. Or our Potion Prep Room as we'd been calling it.

"Angel, I wanted to ask you something. But I was worried Chloe and Jade were having too much fun with the topic, so I figured we could talk in private."

"Let me guess, you want a rundown of Zane's exes? Maybe some sort of witchy background checks on him and his past lovers?"

She caught me off guard with the exes comment. I figured a guy like Zane must have a number of them, but I tried not to focus on it. But if Angel offered up the info, would I really want to know?

"No. No, that's not it at all. I want to know about the Hellions. Why didn't you go to them for help? Don't get me wrong, I'm happy you came to me. But they're demons, wouldn't they have the inside track on all of this?"

It was clear to me that Angel was avoiding eye contact. As I suspected, I'd hit a sensitive topic. "Because...I can't go to them. If they find out I took the Heart of the Phoenix...I hate to think what would happen."

"What is the Heart anyway? What's it made of that makes

it so precious? And why does it matter so much to the Hellions?"

"You know, Emmy, maybe I shouldn't drag you into this. There's so much you don't know."

"I know Zane is missing. And I care about him. I also care about the fact that your parents are missing. That's enough to make me want to help, no matter what."

"All right. If you're in all the way, you deserve to know as much as I can tell you," she said, shifting her glance to the wall of jarred herbs and extracts.

"Mind if I take a few small samples?"

Confused by the oddly sudden change of topics, I shook my head. "Be my guest."

Silently watching her peruse the shelves, my curiosity grew. Once she'd made her selections, she scattered a dusting of each herb across the table. She removed two things from her purse: a tennis ball-sized pink crystal and a small wooden wand. With the tip of the wand, she traced a pentagram in the herbal mixture and placed the crystal in the center.

"I haven't had any luck with my locator spells, but at least I can give you some history on this mess."

Waving the wand in a long slow arc, she chanted in a language which was unfamiliar—perhaps even ancient.

"Now, watch the table as if it was a TV screen. This is a memory spell. It will show you things that are known to me. Or in this case, a memory my mom shared with me. Now, I am going to share it with you. I wish I could use a spell like this to learn what I don't yet know, like where my family is. Or even to locate Dexter. But the magic doesn't work like that."

CHAPTER ELEVEN

A shimmering light appeared on the tabletop. Blurry shapes took on recognizable forms. The glow was accompanied by a crackling sound, like the noise you sometimes hear when trying to tune in an AM radio.

I was about to ask a question when Angel placed her finger over her lips, urging my silence.

Suddenly, the images and sounds became crystal clear. I'm not sure what I had expected. Maybe to watch Angel's memories unfold like some sort of mystical TV show. I never once expected to be magically swept into her memories.

The room was illuminated solely by ethereal green flames from a dozen candles. At first glance, it appeared to be a Victorian era study. The walls were covered in dark oak panels, except for one. It was completely covered by bookshelves. Three figures gathered around an oval table, examining several unfurled scrolls.

A pair of hands stretched a scroll across the table. "Make no mistake, Rockland. Once we do this, there is no turning back." It was a man's voice, and he had a familiar British accent. The weird flickering light finally illuminated his face.

Ash? What's going on?

The second figure was no man. Well, not quite a man. He had a large pair of bat-like wings that slowly expanded and contracted, and he had a long whip of a tail which snaked in feline fashion.

"Yes, your grace. But with the passing of each night, our situation grows more desperate, more miserable...we've truly reached the point where we cannot tolerate it anymore."

Is that Rocky? The Hellion I met at the Hellhole bar and grill? What is he doing there?

"Well, this is Hell after all," a woman replied, her voice dripping with sarcasm. "Desperation and misery seem like the ambience and flavor one would expect, no?"

Stepping into the light, I instantly recognized the woman. She was draped in a long black robe and wearing a classic witch's hat.

Eve? What is going on? I had so many questions for Angel. Hopefully these memories of hers would answer a few of them.

"I suppose." Rocky caressed his long slithering tail. "But a lot of unpleasant behaviors are par for the course in Hell as well. So me asking for a little help with treason, mutiny, or even a bloody coup d'état shouldn't be seen as an outlandish request."

Ash shook his head. "Ixnay on the spilling of blood. And especially not noble blood. Besides, the Marquis D'Phoenix is immortal anyway. It wouldn't really do much good."

"Oh, but how satisfying it would be to impale that son of a bitch on a giant stake, watch him wiggle like a worm on a fishing hook," Rocky replied, gleefully stabbing the air with an invisible stake.

"Jeesh, chill Dracula," Eve said.

"Nobody is getting impaled," Ash said, unrolling another scroll. "Eve created a spell to imprison the Marquis in another dimension. Once he is out of the way, you and your legion will be free to leave Hell. However, terms and conditions apply. Results may vary."

Rocky scurried around the table, leaning his face inches from Ash's. "Conditions? What conditions?"

Ash placed his index finger on Rocky's forehead and gave him a shove. "Quit breathing on me. Eve will give you the specifics."

"Right," Eve said, retrieving a necklace from some hidden place deep within her robes.

Pockets? Nice.

"Let's go over the sequence of events that are needed in order to make this spell work. First, we need to gather the entire legion of Hellions, along with the Marquis. That will be your job. Think you can handle it, Rocky?"

"There's already a general assembly on the schedule for later this week. So, there you go. Easy peasy lemon squeezy."

Eve whipped out her wand like a seasoned gunslinger drawing on her target. "Easy what? What was that? A spell? A curse? Are you trying to hex me?"

Rocky stumbled backward, trying to get some distance from the business end of Eve's wand. "No, it's—it's just—just a saying-the people condemned to Hell came up with. I suppose I hate it myself, but you have to admit, it's kind of catchy."

"So is smallpox," Eve growled.

"Back to the plan. After you and the Hellions are gathered with the Marquis, I will invoke the spell which will banish him to another realm. Once this happens, all Hellions present at the time will be released from Hell. The conditions are as follows; you will live on Earth in human form. There, you will establish a colony in a magical forest near my farm."

"Farm? We're hardly farmers."

"Think of yourselves as my private army, protecting me

and the forest. But for all intents and purposes, you will be free to live your lives as you wish. I don't care what you do for work or for pleasure, just be there should I ever call on you. There are some other perks for the Hellions. You will have full access to all of the forest's interdimensional portals, and on every full moon, you will shift into your demonic forms."

"Sounds like something we could get behind. What's with that pendant?" Rocky asked, pointing to the necklace.

"With witchcraft, every spell requires the creation of a reversing remedy. In essence, it's an emergency fail-safe."

"Ah, a second spell which can be used to reverse the effects of the original spell. Got it."

"Exactly. But considering the risks, we need to keep the reversing remedy in a safe place where only the three of us know its location. The spell for the remedy will be etched into the back of this turquoise scarab pendant and then hidden." Eve turned the pendant over in her hand.

"A safe place? I don't know about that." Rocky shrugged. "Do any of us trust each other enough for one person to hold on to it? I mean, in a pinch, anyone might find it useful."

"That's why we leave it to one of Hell's most effective and discreet guardians, a hellhound," Ash said. "And I just happen to have one at my disposal."

"Hmmm. You mean like an actual hellhound? If you have one, I like that idea better than one of you holding the pendant. Or even one of my fellow Hellions for that matter. But I want to be present when you give it to your hellhound. Sorry, but I don't trust anyone these days," Rocky replied.

"Fine by me," Ash agreed.

"Then it's settled. I'll cast the spell during the general assembly," Eve said.

The memory trip fast forwarded in a blur until it picked up again in a new location. We found ourselves in some sort of great hall.

It was dark, gothic, and scary, with gargoyles perched from the tops of black marble columns. Shiny dark green tile floors and gray marble walls added to the gloomy look. The orange light from giant flaming geysers of lava shone through the purple and dark red, stained-glass windows, providing the sole light for the interior.

Honestly, it was beyond creepy. The only other way I can describe it would be to call it a hellish, perverse version of a cathedral.

It started with a clicking sound of goats' hooves on the tile. But as hundreds of bat-winged Hellions filed in, the clicking of their hooves echoed through the hall until the noise became nearly unbearable.

A thin man with a long, well-groomed beard stepped out onto the stage at one end of the hall. His hair was impeccable, and he wore a neat business suit. His black framed glasses completed his trendy big-tech corporate look.

"Good morning, everyone. I trust you all had a safe and fulfilling weekend. Especially those who partook in the Building a Love Bond with Your Inner Devil Yoga Retreat. Personally, I spent a rewarding weekend meditating in a Navajo sweat lodge."

The Hellions squirmed, and their collective snarling was enough to get the Marquis to pause and take note.

"Okay then. Looking forward to this week, we will hold a safety fair on Tuesday which will mesh well with this month's theme of reducing our fire and brimstone footprint. On Thursday, we will be holding a very timely legion-wide training program called 'You can't say that, can you?' Our guest speaker will be Norma Sass, author of the best-selling self-help book titled 'Speak of the Devil—A Demon's Guide to Sensitive and Respectful Communication.' I know it will be a fulfilling day."

A loud collective groan rose up from the legion. A few

Hellions shouted their complaints. "When's the next orgy? We haven't had one in months!" and "We need to get back to raiding! Our neighbors aren't going to plunder themselves!" and few shouts which made no sense to me as they seemed like physical impossibilities, such as "Go fuck yourself!"

"I know change is often difficult, but in the months since assuming the role as your Marquis D'Phoenix, I would like to think we have achieved tremendous growth as a community. Responsible, sensitive denizens of Hell and good stewards of our environment. Oh, and don't forget IT will be holding pre-meeting planning meetings slated for Friday to prepare for the meetings which will prepare us for updating our computer user agreements."

Eve suddenly appeared on the stage, maybe it would be more accurate to say she angrily stomped onto the stage. "I think I've heard enough torturous garbage."

Suspending the scarab pendant high from her outstretched arm, she silently mumbled.

"Wait!" the Marquis protested. "Our Demonic Relations department is fully staffed and certified in handling whistle-blower complaints! They'd be happy to assist you with—"

"Bye," Eve said, her closed lip smile curled with evil satisfaction.

"No! I just ordered new cubicles and work centers!" he cried.

Then, in a little puff of green smoke, which smelled like boiled cabbage and diesel fumes, he disappeared.

The joyous Hellions cheered wildly, several of them took to the air, flapping around the hall in an impromptu celebratory display.

CHAPTER TWELVE

*A*ngel tapped my shoulder and shrugged. My guess was she was wondering if I'd seen enough of her memories to understand how everything went down in Hell.

I nodded. I understood the importance of the pendant and how everything was connected, and where her parents fit into the scenario.

She waved her wand, and we were once again standing in the back storeroom.

"And that's how it went down with the Hellions, the Marquis, and my parents. Can you see why the pendant is so important, and why I'd be in deep crap if anyone knows I took it?"

"I completely understand, but there's one thing I'm. not sure I get. How did you get the pendant in the first place, and where did you hide it?"

"I snuck into Dexter's lair. He was already missing, so I figured it was the perfect time to snag the pendant. I hid it at the entrance to a portal."

"At the entrance to a portal?" I asked, thinking about my

afternoon swim at the magical glen. "Would that be at the bottom of a magical spring fed pond in the forest?" I asked.

"That's exactly where it is. How did you know?"

"Zane took me to that glen. After it transformed into a picture-perfect tropical oasis, I dove in for a swim. I saw something down at the bottom. Huh. It's hard to believe a place so beautiful was actually at the threshold to Hell. Anyway, do you think it's still there?"

"It was a few days ago. We should check it today. But, for now, let's check out your collection of grimoires."

"My...what?" I asked, befuddled by her suggestion. "I'm not a witch. Our remedy books are just angelic recipe books, nothing more."

"Someday, you'll realize your 'angelic recipes' are just another type of magic. But for now, your books don't really interest me. I know for a fact that Midge left you quite a collection of witchcraft approved spell books here. Those are the ones we need right now," Angel said, opening a cardboard box filled with Midge's antique books we'd kept in storage.

"Hold on a sec. Midge left a lot of antique books in this store, but are you saying she specifically maintained a collection of witch's spell books?"

"That's exactly what I'm saying." She blew the dust off a tattered, moth-eaten, old leather-bound book.

"You seem surprised. Which is, in turn, surprising to me."

"It's just—"

I didn't know what information I should disclose. The cat was already out of the bag about our angelic identity, at least to Zane and his family, but that didn't mean I shouldn't be cautious. Still, I had so many questions about Midge.

"I guess Midge had a whole life that we didn't know anything about. It's all so mysterious," I said, dragging out a second box full of books.

"I think everyone should have a little mystery about them. Makes them interesting."

"I suppose you have a point." I opened the box.

"Do you know why she collected those books? Was she into the occult or something?"

"It was a lucrative business for her. The right clients will pay a lot of money for a rare grimoire because they know the true value."

"So, she catered to witches then?"

"Mostly. My mom always saw herself as Midge's exclusive client and personal grimoire concierge," Angel said, leafing through the yellowed pages of a handwritten tome. "Fact is, though, Midge would sell to anyone."

I remembered the book Ash bought. "Some of Midge's old books are stocked out on the shelves in the store. Your dad bought one of them when we first met. It had a very unusual title, The Lesser Key of Solomon. Do you know if that was one of those witch's spell books?"

"I've heard of it. It's actually one used in necromancy, and it's supposed to have instructions for conjuring up specific demons. Basically, it's the white pages of Hell. That's probably why Dad wanted it. But it is the sort of book I'm looking for now," Angel said, closing the box. "There's nothing helpful in this one. Have you sold any more of Midge's books? To anyone?"

Pausing to recall any sales, I shook my head. "No. I'd remember if I did."

But there was something else that I'd remembered. The receipt I'd found in Mike's studio. "Hold on." I hurried over to the desk.

Rifling through a drawer, I plucked out the evidence.

"We found this in Mike's studio. Apparently, he paid Midge a steep price for some old book. Do you think it means anything?"

Angel quickly grabbed the receipt and closely examined it.

"Le Dragon Rouge. Also known as The Red Dragon. It's a very rare grimoire. Mom told me about this book. She said it was impossible to find a copy, but we should always keep an eye out for one. And by the looks of it, Midge found one. And sold it to...a damn postcard photographer? What the hell, Midge?"

"Besides the book being so rare, what makes it so special?"

"It's a collection of banned magic, dark magic, if you will. If a spell exists to control a hellhound, it's exactly the kind of grimoire we'd find it in."

Her eyes suddenly widened and flashed with excitement.

"He actually bought the book."

Flattening the little scrap of paper, she suddenly gasped with a realization.

"I bet that book is still there, in his studio. It just might contain a hellhound control spell. We find Dexter, we find my family. Odds are slim, but still—"

"Unfortunately, it isn't there," I said, breaking midstream into her rambling sentence. "We went all through that place."

I watched as her excitement drained like air from a leaky balloon.

"Sorry."

"Damn it! Then all we can do is run with yet another assumption. Mike knew that book contained something powerful, and he used it to control Dexter. Whoever has it, now has Dexter, Zane, Mom, and Dad," Angel said, slumping down to the floor.

"What do we do now?" The panic attack building up inside her caused her voice to quiver.

"Okay, here's the deal. That Red Dragon book is gone. We don't have a clue to its location. But we do know where that magic scarab is. We go to the glen and get that necklace. That's exactly what we do next," I said, doing my best to calm her down by at least sounding confident and determined— even if it was nothing more than an act.

"Okay." She nodded. "Who knows, maybe that charm carries a magical link to Dexter or even my mom. I might be able to pick up on it."

"Right. Besides, if Dexter is under someone else's control, he isn't going to fall for your trap anyway. We can't just leave it out there. What if it finds its way into the wrong hands? And if he isn't under someone's spell, maybe he is just roaming free. Who knows? He might have found his way through the portal. Zane and your parents might be with him already. In any case, we'll take this one step at a time."

"Are you always this optimistic?"

"No, but I'm working toward it," I said, beaming from what I took as a compliment.

"They have a saying in Heaven. 'To succeed, the only thing you need is a positive attitude'. I think there's a lot of truth to it."

A closed lipped smile appeared on Angel's face and her eyes sparkled with mischief. "Well, us witches also have a saying. 'Sometimes all you need is a positive attitude, and a sharp knife'. I'll go with that."

CHAPTER THIRTEEN

"Rope, flashlights, water, glow sticks, and an old compass," I said, double checking my backpack.

"Wand," Angel said, checking her back pocket. "That's all I'll need."

Chloe and Jade rushed into the shop. They huffed, catching their breath. "Guess what? We have a new clue. Last night was open Mike night," Chloe said.

"Autopsy, Chloe. It was Mike's fricking autopsy, not 'open Mike night'. You sure have been saying weird stuff lately," Jade groaned.

"Same thing. Anyways, Mike's death only appeared to be from a heart attack. Upon further examination, he didn't have any physical damage to his heart or blood vessels."

Jade jumped in, adding, "Yeah, it's like his heart just stopped. Like, for no reason."

"Huh. That doesn't mean he was murdered." I shrugged. "It just means his cause of death hasn't been determined."

"Do you know if they got a toxicology report back yet?" Angel asked.

Chloe and Jade stared at each other, like a pair of puppies

who just heard a confusing new sound. "Uh, taxi, toxi, something or another. Daryl and Erik were talking about that same thing. What was it they found out?" Chloe asked.

"It was about digits or something. I don't know. It was all medicinal gibberish to me," Jade replied.

"Digits? Hold on," Angel said, alerted by something Jade had said. "Does the word digitalis sound familiar?"

"Yeah, maybe," Chloe replied, and Jade nodded.

"What does it mean?" I asked.

"It means Mike Schmitz was murdered with a deadly poison called digitalis. With the right dosage, it stops the heart, making it appear like the victim suffered a heart attack."

"Jeesh, that sounds exotic. Where would someone get a hold of a crazy thing like that?" I asked, hoping it would narrow the list of possible suspects.

"Actually, it's quite common. It's an extract of the foxglove plant which I bet you can find in at least a dozen flower beds around Angel Bay."

She was right. I'd seen plenty of the beautiful blue and purple shade loving flowers growing just along main street.

"So, anyone could get their hands on it. Great." I sighed, closing my backpack. Then I remembered where else I'd seen foxglove plants growing—Eve's herb garden. With Angel present, the timing wasn't right to start adding her or her mom to our list of suspects.

"We'll look into that next. We have something else to take care of now. Get some hiking clothes on, girls, we're heading into the forest to retrieve the Heart of the Phoenix."

Two hours later, we were hiking the same trail Zane and I took to visit the magical glen.

"I don't see what the big deal is about this place," Chloe said, her hands on her hips. Her face twisted with disgust when she looked down at the muddy, weed-choked spring.

"I'm sure this would seem like paradise…if you were a frog. Is that what Zane turned out to be? Some kind of demonic amphibian?" Jade said, joining Chloe on the edge of the spring.

"He most likely turned into a horny toad," Chloe added, cracking herself up.

Noticing the leaves had begun to glimmer, I gave Angel a knowing smile. "Three, two, one," I whispered.

Right on the mark, the mosquito-infested mudhole transformed into the amazing tropical pool I'd seen in my previous visit.

Angel stripped off her clothes and dove in before Jade's and Chloe's surprised mouths could form a sentence.

"She's diving down to get a magical scarab necklace from the pool," I explained.

Our eyes were fixed on Angel as she swam gracefully down to the bottom.

"Now that we have a minute alone, I want to let you know of another place I saw foxgloves growing—in Eve's garden."

Jade shrugged her shoulders. "So what? Mike was poisoned with a common flower which was available to anyone. It doesn't mean much."

"Maybe not, but it takes more than picking a flower to kill someone with it. It takes knowledge. I mean, come on, did you know those flowers were a deadly poison which can mimic a heart attack?"

"Angel knew all about that flower. But she seemed as surprised as anyone that Mike Schmitz was dead," Chloe said, her voice trailing off into space like it does when she gets lost in her own thoughts. "Maybe the killer is a florist."

"Or…" Jade dramatically waved her index finger. "Maybe the killer is a witch who knows all about using flowering plants to carry out sinister deeds. Not saying it was Angel. But Eve is more likely to know about killing someone with a flower than your average garden variety, yoga-pants-wearing, Angel Bay dog walker."

Angel surfaced with a splash, and I handed her a towel from my backpack. "Did you get it?"

"No," she said, wrapping herself in the towel. "It's...I can't believe it, but it's...."

A branch snapped in the nearby clump of trees. Just as we all turned to look, two men stepped out of the shadows. It was Rocky and another Hellion.

"Hands up! No sudden moves. Looking for this?" he said, dangling the pendant from one hand and flashing a shiny black pistol in the other. Turning to a younger, blonde haired Hellion to his left, he pointed the barrel of his gun at Angel's clothes pile. "Buddy, go grab her things."

The handsome young man made a dry gulping sound, like he'd just swallowed a rock. His gaze shifted nervously between Angel, the clothes, and Rocky. "Wha-what?"

"You heard me, boy. Her clothes. Go get 'em. You scared or something?" Rocky barked.

"Yeah, Buddy. Are you scared of me?" Angel said, boldly taunting the young Hellion. Her eyes burned into him like lasers.

"N—n—no," he mumbled, stepping forward like he was navigating a minefield. "Uh, I'm sorry about this, Angel."

"If you touch my clothes, you should be scared. I've always liked you, Buddy. It'd be a real shame to turn a sweet snack like you into a toad."

"You...you always liked me? Hell, I didn't know you even noticed me. I don't suppose there's a chance you'd go with me to the Dairy Fairy for a sundae after this?"

"Dude. She just threatened to turn you into a toad," Chloe groaned.

Buddy looked over his shoulder. "What do you want her

clothes for anyway? Ain't none of us gonna fit into them tiny things."

"Damn it, boy. Just get her wand. It's got to be in that pile of clothes."

Buddy scurried closer and quickly found Angel's wand which had been tucked into her pocket.

"Okay, I'm disarmed. Now, tell me, what are you doing with the scarab, and what do you fools want from us?" Angel asked.

"Hey!" Rocky waved his gun. "We aren't just your average everyday fools."

"Aren't we lucky, we get the Sunday specials," Angel said, accompanied by a chorus of laughter from Chloe and Jade.

"We heard about all the sightings of a hellhound at large in Angel Bay. It made us a little nervous that it could be your daddy's dog, meaning nobody was guarding the scarab. Your parents and brother seem to have dropped off the face of the Earth too. So, we were about to jump through the portal to investigate and look what we found." Rocky swung the pendant in a loop. "It was just sitting at the bottom of the pond, all alone. So, I grabbed it. We also heard about some dead guy. And now, thanks to listening to you and your friends, we find out he was whacked. And we ain't goin' down for that."

"Can we put our hands down yet?" I asked, hoping to diffuse the tension. "We aren't going to do anything."

"You're Zane's girl, ain't ya? Ever since you and your weird friends came to town, things have been getting bizarre."

"Says the guy who grows bat wings on the full moon," Jade replied.

Rocky leaned close enough for me to smell his garlicky breath. "Who, and what, are you anyway?"

"They're friends of the family. Not to mention, powerful witches. You're skating on thin ice, Rocky. I suggest you put away your little pea shooter and take things down a notch so we can talk this over." She smiled at Buddy and adjusted her towel.

I actually think she may have flashed him.

A pair of shiny black horns erupted from Buddy's hair. His face turned as red as a baboon's backside.

"Oh man," he groaned, frantically trying to conceal his horns with his hands.

Rocky turned around, drawn by Buddy's antics. "Really? Control yourself, man."

Angel chanted a string of ancient words. When she shouted, "Now!" her wand flew from Buddy's sweaty grip into her hands.

Chloe, Jade, and I rushed Rocky and tackled him to the ground. To our relief, the pistol turned out to be nothing more than a plastic toy.

Angel snagged the scarab and leveled her wand at Rocky. "This wand isn't a toy. What color toads do you idiots prefer to be?"

"Angel, please don't hurt them. We're all on the same side here," I pleaded.

"Fine. Let him up," Angel said.

Chloe shifted her body and straddled Rocky's chest while Jade squealed excitedly and stretched his arms over his head.

"No way!" Chloe panted. "Finally, I've got a dirty talking Alpha just like the ones in my favorite erotica shifter MC series. Come on, Rocky, say something deliciously filthy."

"What the actual fuck is wrong with you? Get your ass off me!" he shouted.

"Not exactly the hot panty-melting verbiage typical of erotic fantasy writing," Chloe said, reluctantly sliding off him.

"It's disappointing, actually." Jade stood up and brushed the dust from her clothes.

"Excuse my friends, they grew up as feral children and

haven't completed their socialization therapy yet," I said, apologetically.

"Down! Bad girls!" I shouted, smacking them with a fern.

Finally separated, we all sat quietly at the edge of the pond. We told Rocky and Buddy everything we knew about Dexter, Mike Schmitz, and Angel's missing family.

"So, we were thinking, this scarab might help us locate them," Angel said, turning the little charm in her hand.

"I can't let you keep that. The Hellions have too much to lose," Rocky said, taking the necklace back. "Sorry. And who knows, all of this might have already reversed the spell. The Marquis could even be on his way back as we speak. We're returning this to Dexter's lair."

"I get it. You're worried about the Marquis and we're worried for my family," Angel sighed. "We can't be going at each other's throats. We have to trust each other. If you'll go through the portal and search on the other side, we'll try to pin down the other leads we've got here."

Rocky's answer was short and quick. "No deal. We all go together. And that means every single one of us here."

CHAPTER FOURTEEN

"*I* don't know about this, Angel." My voice quivered as I whispered into her ear. "Zane described these portals as doorways to Hell. I'm pretty sure Heaven is going to frown on this."

"Relax. I've seen you girls in action. You guys have already rung up a list of devilish behavior to atone for. What's another charge? Besides, can you think of another place to start searching for Zane?"

"I guess you're right," I said, relenting to my fate.

News of Zane's disappearance left a big aching hole in my heart, and I'd been patching it over by working on solving the mystery. But instead of things coming into focus, the whole mess seemed bigger and blurrier than ever.

"I know you're nervous and worried. So am I. Just stick with me," she replied.

"Everyone, hold hands!" Rocky bellowed.

Noticing Chloe clasping her hands together, he shook his head in dismay. "Each other's hands, for Pete's sake!"

Satisfied we'd followed his basic instructions, he continued, "I'll open the portal and count down. Jump through when I say. He waved his arm over the pool, chanting what sounded like unintelligible gibberish. The crystal-clear water transformed into a swirling dark-green fog.

"This is the portal. Get ready to jump," Angel said.

Rocky looked down the line of us and shouted, "Three! Two! One! Now!"

We jumped, except for Chloe, who was simply dragged into the maelstrom by Jade's strong grip.

We landed on our feet while she rolled through the sand and came to rest against a large rock.

"I told you to jump when I said so," Rocky scolded her.

"I was waiting, but you never said jump," Chloe whined, wobbling to her feet.

I spun around, taking in our hot, dry surroundings. It looked the same in every direction—barren, sandy, and void of any life. And everything, including the sky, had a sickly pink hue to it. Visibility was low, and it was difficult to see where the land ended, and the sky began.

"You know what? This looks a lot like those pictures sent back by the Mars rover," Jade said.

"Well, it ain't Mars. Welcome to Purgatory, ladies," Rocky said.

Remarkably, he and Buddy had transformed into their true Hellion form—bat wings, tail, and horns.

"There's nothing out here. How do we even know which way to go?" I asked.

"This way," Angel said, leading the way, alongside Rocky and Buddy.

"If I knew we were going on a hike through the deserts of Hell, I'd have worn something other than flip-flops," Jade groaned.

"Purgatory, actually," Buddy pointed out.

"Well, Purgatory actually sucks," Chloe added.

We trudged through the hot sand for nearly a half hour before we saw something take shape in front of us.

"Oh my God! We are not climbing that. I'm not climbing that," Chloe said.

It was a large outcropping of rock which formed a natural wall. At nearly a hundred feet tall and stretching as far as I could see, it seemed like an impenetrable barrier.

"The end of the proverbial road?" I asked.

"Give him a minute," Angel said, pointing to Rocky.

Rocky scurried along the face of the wall until he settled on a particular stone. Slowly turning it like it was a combination lock, he listened carefully.

"Bingo!" he shouted as a cavernous opening appeared.

At any other time, the cool, musty cave would've been uninviting to say the least. But considering the hellish hike we'd just completed, it was an unlikely oasis.

"Look!" Jade said, pointing to the walls and ceiling. In the dark, thousands of glowing spots created a dazzling greenish blue lightshow which revealed the path ahead.

"It's beautiful." I gasped.

"Glowworms," Angel said. "Millions of them live in here. Come on, it's only a few hundred yards to Dexter's lair."

"I meant to ask you something. Zane told me there was a penalty for removing anything from the enchanted forest, like a curse. Does that apply to removing the scarab from Dexter's lair?"

"Yeah, I'm sure it does. I'm only hoping the punishment involved unleashed Dexter and not something worse."

Neither of us wanted to say what we were most worried about out loud. That perhaps Zane, Ash, and Eve weren't being held by some twisted sorcerer but, in fact, had paid the ultimate penalty for Angel's removal of the scarab.

"This is Dexter's lair," Rocky said.

I guess I expected to walk into someplace a bit more

frightening, you know, more fitting for a hellhound's lair. Perhaps I imagined there would be piles of gnawed up bones, fur, and God knows what else.

Instead, there was a huge blue dog bed, complete with a king-sized mattress. It was topped with a thick gray comforter and a few decorative accent pillows. Scattered across Dexter's bed was a collection of plush dog toys, including the cutest pink unicorn I'd ever seen.

A spring fed watering trough and a pile of warm glowing stones turned the cave into a perfectly comfortable dog's den.

"Huh!" Pretty much summed up my reaction to what I saw.

"And I'm putting the Heart of the Phoenix right back where it belongs," Rocky said, stuffing it under Dexter's bed.

"Will that be enough to reverse a curse, if it did break a curse?" I asked.

"I have no idea," Angel whispered. "All we can do now is look around the lair to see if we can find any clues. Any signs, at all, that Zane or my parents have been here."

"You witches better hope you didn't screw up big time. Stealing the Heart of the Phoenix was a real bonehead move," Rocky snapped.

"Hey! We're ang—" Jade nearly blew our cover with Rocky and Buddy. Thankfully, Angel cut her off.

"Shhh." Angel waved her hand, signaling for everyone to lower their volume. "Dexter isn't the only hellhound in these caverns. There's a whole pack of them."

"Hellhounds might be the least of our worries. There's all kinds of creepy critters lurking in here," Buddy whispered, his wings and tail twitched nervously with every syllable he uttered.

"When will we know if returning the scarab worked?" I asked.

Rocky shrugged his big bat wings. "Everything we're

doing here is based on a hunch. My only concern is getting Dexter back to guard this necklace and keep the Marquis in exile. I couldn't care less about your family."

"Bu..but that's not what you said be...before," Buddy said, cocking his head. "You...you were all worried about Eve. You were a mess."

"Whoa." Angel was physically taken aback by Buddy's words. "Maybe you ought to explain yourself, Rocky. Do you have some sort of romantic attraction to my mom?"

"Who? Me?" Rocky scrunched up his face, over-exaggerating his surprised reaction to her allegation.

"Of course not. I'm only concerned for her safety because she is the witch who exiled the Marquis, and she's our patron on Earth."

"Huh?" Buddy's confusion was genuine and innocent. "Then why have you been talking about how much you like Eve for months?"

Rocky threw his hands out and shook his head. But he didn't exactly deny it.

"What kinds of things has he been saying?" Angel asked.

"I dunno. Like, how hot she is. And he wished Ash didn't show up because it totally messed up the thing him and Eve had going," Buddy said.

"Oh yeah, and he said something else about her. He said, 'The rustier the roof, the wetter the basement'. But I don't know what that's about."

"Busted. But hey, what can I say? I'm attracted to hot redheads. And your mom has a thing for demons," Rocky scoffed.

Angel made a weird growling sound and readied her wand. "Sick bastard."

"Angel, please don't do anything rash. It seems to me that every sudden decision has resulted in one tragic consequence after another. Let's not add to it," I said.

"Listen to your friend, Angel. She's right."

"Fine." Angel leveled her wand at Rocky, taking aim at his forehead. "But if I find out you've been trying to get my dad out of the picture so you can get back with my mom, I'll fricking vaporize you. Am I being clear enough?"

"Crystal."

"Wow. It's like a love triangle movie you'd see on one of those romantic Wifetime channels. You know, where the old boyfriend comes back to the small town and rekindles his love affair with his baby momma, pushing the bad-boy lover to the sidelines," Chloe said.

Jade shook her head. "No, it's more like a true crime drama being played out in real time. Jilted lover wipes out family in a fit of jealous rage, surviving daughter goes on revenge killing spree."

"Let's all hope it turns out to be more like Chloe's version than Jade's," Angel replied.

I picked up on a faint noise. It sounded like someone running through puddles of water after a storm. The splash started deep in the cavern and grew closer by the second.

"Listen," I said, cupping my ear. "Someone is coming."

"Or something," Buddy said, scurrying up the side of the cave wall.

In the weird ethereal glowworm light, I could make out the shape of a man running closer. "Emmy?" a voice called out.

I knew instantly that it was Zane's voice.

"Zane!"

Racing up to me, he lifted me off my feet and kissed me.

"How did you get down here?" I asked.

"It wasn't on purpose. I was out hunting the forest for Dexter and my dad. Next thing I know, I was sucked into a vortex. I landed in a labyrinth, where I was trapped until now. Finally, a path opened up and I was able to find my way here."

"I guess that answers the question. The curse for me removing the Heart of the Phoenix was Zane's imprisonment," Angel said.

"Wait. What did you do?"

"Dexter was already missing. So, I came here and stole the Heart of the Phoenix. I thought that if I kept Dexter on the loose, it would keep Dad around while he searched for him. My plan kind of worked. I didn't realize you'd end up paying the price. Sorry. But it's back here in Dexter's lair now, so at least you're free. I just wish I knew where Mom and Dad were."

"Mom is missing too?" Zane asked.

"And I had nothing to do with it!" Rocky shouted, preemptively declaring his innocence. "In fact, I'll prove it. You all can look for Ash, Eve, and Dexter. I'm staying right here to guard the Heart of the Phoenix until Dexter returns."

"It's all such a mess, Zane. Now that the scarab is back in place and we found you, we need to get back to Angel Bay and sort the rest of this out."

"We even have a murder to solve," I added.

"I'll help you find your parents, Angel," Buddy said, empathetically taking her hand. It was clear to anyone that he was sweet on her, and he felt bad for how things had been going.

"Thanks, Buddy."

CHAPTER FIFTEEN

"*B*ack to the drawing board."

I set a shoebox stuffed full of Midge's old receipts on the table.

"We know Midge sold a very powerful grimoire, Le Dragon Rouge, to Mike Schmitz. My guess is he used this spell book to conjure up Dexter, and he somehow figured out how to use Dexter's mind control powers to carry out his blackmail scheme."

Angel removed a handful of receipts and examined them under the light.

"Right. That particular grimoire is rare enough, and as I've said before, some obscure photographer isn't going to know it could be used to conjure a hellhound to do his bidding. Unless Mike was a supernatural, he wouldn't even know about grimoires or hellhounds."

"So...we've been looking at this all wrong?" Jade asked.

"Mike Schmitz may not really be the ultimate villain here. He may have been a pawn in a larger scheme."

"I don't follow what you are saying, Jade. We found the

photos in his shop. I thought it was obvious he was the villain," Chloe said.

"I'm not saying he didn't carry out the caper. I'm just saying that maybe he was working on behalf of someone who was familiar with the grimoire and the dark arts," she replied.

"Good theory. He could have been under their control, or perhaps he was a willing accomplice," I added.

"Either way, whoever that other person is most likely has possession of the grimoire, Dexter, and probably my parents," Zane said.

"Don't forget he or she also murdered Mike Schmitz," I said. "Probably because he served his purpose, or was no longer willing to cooperate. If we can solve the murder mystery, we solve everything. Hopefully."

"So, what are we doing with all of these receipts?" Chloe asked.

"I was thinking. Who else besides Ash and Eve would be in the market for those spell books? Mike Schmitz bought one, but who else. If we can find another buyer, we have a prime suspect."

"Good point, Emmy. Hey Buddy, would you run and pick up some coffees for everyone. We're going to need the caffeine." Angel handed Buddy some cash and had him take our orders.

Zane divided the receipts into even piles—more or less. "Then let's get busy."

By mid-afternoon we'd reviewed every single receipt.

"Here are the grand totals for sales of grimoires, magical recipe books, or anything related to the occult. Eve bought a total of thirty-two books, Ash bought twenty-one, and Mike Schmitz purchased just the one. None of Midge's customers had any interest in the subject. And she appears to have kept meticulous sales records," I said.

Chloe removed her glasses, giving us a little wave. "Well, it's a darn good thing Midge didn't sell Ash any of her shoes."

"Huh?" Once again, Chloe had me completely befuddled.

"Yeah, because otherwise, she would have sold her sole to the devil! Get it? Like soul, but sole. It's a pun or whatever," she laughed so hard she snorted. "I really crack myself up sometimes."

Angel closed the shoebox and shoved it across the table. "Damn it. Another dead end. That didn't help a lick. Maybe we ought to take a break and think this over some more."

Zane stretched. "I spent the night playing hide and seek from a minotaur in a labyrinth. I'm beat, but I'd feel too guilty to sleep, knowing Mom and Dad might need our help."

"Do you want to go upstairs and lay down just for a bit? Get some rest?" I whispered. I would've loved to have him join me in bed for a little afternoon snuggle. But considering the circumstances, I didn't think it would be right to even suggest it.

"I should, but I don't think I can rest until I know that Mom and Dad are safe. Raincheck, babe?" Zane kissed me on the cheek.

I was pretty sure he understood my hopes to share some time alone.

Angel slumped over the table. "Come on, Zane. We're completely useless right now. Do you care if I take your couch for a catnap, Emmy?"

"We all need a break. Besides, Jade and I are going to catch lunch with Erik and Daryl," Chloe said. "We'll meet back here in two hours?"

"And I'll walk the town to see if Dexter left a trail for me to track," Buddy said.

Angel and Zane followed me upstairs to the apartment. Angel found the couch and a blanket, passing out almost immediately.

"Come with me," I whispered, leading him to my room.

"These clothes are so dusty," he said, stripping down. Once he got in bed, I curled up next to him, my hand resting on his bare chest. He fell asleep within a minute.

I, however, was wide awake. My mind decided that I needed an X-rated slide show of all the things we'd done over the weekend. And it made me crave more.

Your timing is awful and inconsiderate. Just leave him be. I was actually scolding myself into behaving.

Concentrate on the case. Not Zane.

And that's precisely what I did. I needed to look at everything as if I was an outsider, without any bias.

This entire case hinged on the knowledge of the supernatural. The receipts gave us an indication of the only people in Angel Falls who had that knowledge. Mike Schmitz, Ash, and Eve. Due to the unfortunate passing of Mike, it only left Ash and Eve. And they were missing. Maybe the time had come to quit guessing at a motive and stick with the clues.

A million and one different questions buzzed around in my mind. Questions that could severely impact my relationship with both Zane and his sister. I couldn't help but wonder, though.

Could Ash and Eve be behind any of this? Did I know them well enough to say a demon and a witch aren't capable of murder and blackmail? No, of course not. I'd have to keep them in mind as possible suspects, even if I don't mention it out loud.

Ugh. I hated to think badly of Ash and Eve. Despite my early misgivings with Eve, I'd come to appreciate her honesty when it came to all things Zane. I understood her worry for her son. Since then, we've gotten along just fine. As for Ash, he's always been nice to me and treated me with kindness and respect.

Zane's chest slowly rose and fell with each breath he took, and I felt his heartbeat against the palm of my hand.

He's right here. Completely naked. Deliciously naked.

I closed my eyes and relished the graphic memories from the weekend.

This is crazy. I can't even think straight right now.

My libido seemed to be on overdrive with Zane stretched out beside me. Everything I'd ever read in any of my wicked Dark Beasts books always had the women taking matters into their own hands, so to speak. Maybe this was supposed to be one of those times in our story.

I softly traced my fingers over Zane's sculpted torso. Following the sexy little valley down the center of his abdomen, my hand slipped below the covers. Sliding under the sheet, my fingers gently wrapped around him. Marveling as he swelled and hardened in my hand. I began to stroke him as I lightly kissed his chest. My tongue followed the same path my hand had taken until I made love to him with my mouth.

Zane lazily stroked my hair, and when I finally turned my head to look up at him, he smiled, and his glowing eyes half opened. "Don't stop on my account," he whispered.

"Mmm hmm," I hummed, and continued on with what I had been doing.

It wasn't too long before I sensed his passion growing more urgent. But my body begged me for more. Sweeping aside the hem of my dress, I straddled him.

"I hope this is okay." I felt like I should at least ask for permission.

"I can't think of a better way to wake up." Zane's hands latched onto my hips.

What happened over the course of the next half hour was simply magical, and everything my body had begged me for—and then some.

"Sorry," I whispered as I collapsed beside him. "Kind of."

"Don't be."

"No, really. It was selfish of me. I should've let you sleep longer. And with everything going on..."

"I'm not complaining," he replied, pulling me close.

Melting in the comfort of his embrace, and the afterglow of making love, I knew our relationship had reached an entirely new level. I couldn't imagine life moving forward from that point without him.

The familiar sounds of my friends' voices and laughter drifted up from the store below, as if they were already knocking on my door with terrible timing.

"Already?" I groaned, and reluctantly pried myself out of bed. "We ought to get moving. If their previous behavior is a predictor, they'll be stampeding through the door at any minute."

When we returned downstairs, Chloe, Jade, and Angel were gathered in front of a large whiteboard. They'd scrawled a poorly organized summary of crimes, suspects, and motives with a rainbow of dry-erase markers.

Zane squinted, looking over the board from a variety of angles. "What's that mess supposed to be, modern art?"

"It's a crime solving board, smartass. Just like the detectives use in the movies. This way, we can organize our thoughts. As you can see, we've color coded everything," Chloe replied, quickly wiping off some green scribble and replacing it with red.

Angel tapped the board. "Suffice to say, we suck at being detectives."

One name on the suspect list I noticed they had included was Rocky's.

"This is great. But what we need is something new. A clue."

Just then, as if the hand of fate responded to my request, an empty paper coffee cup rolled off the table.

But it wasn't the nimble hand of fate, it was the butterfingered paws of Buddy. "Sorry. Just trying to clean up our mess."

I couldn't believe I'd overlooked it. The very coffee cups he gathered up were an identical match to the paper cup Mike Schmitz had dropped the night he died.

"Where did you get the coffee from?" I asked.

"That little bakery joint up the street, Kathy's Café," he replied.

Without another word, I bolted out of the room. Sliding to a stop by the wastepaper basket next to the cash register, I was relieved to find the very cup I'd picked up from the scene and discarded in our shop.

"Check this out," I said proudly, returning to the back room.

"This is the cup Mike Schmitz dropped the night he died. Notice that it is identical to the cups Buddy got at Kathy's. Right down to the unique plaid pattern printed on it."

Angel shrugged dismissively. "All that means is Mike Schmitz bought a drink at Kathy's."

"We were thinking about how Mike Schmitz could have ingested the digitalis poison. Maybe it was in whatever he was drinking when he collapsed," I said. "This cup could be our next big clue."

"What do you plan to do? Take it to a crime lab?" Angel replied.

"Nope. Hey, Chloe, remember that process we found in one of our books? The one we used to identify unknown herbs and extracts?"

Chloe removed a large volume of angelic remedies from the bookshelf. "I've got it right here."

"Nice grimoire," Angel said, leafing through the book.

"It's not a grimoire. It's our Angelic Remedy Book," Chloe snapped, lifting her chin.

Clearly, she had taken offense to Angel's insinuation that we were somehow involved in witchcraft.

"I keep telling you girls, it's the same damn thing," Angel replied.

Inserting myself between them, I wanted to act quickly to prevent the escalation of an argument.

"As angels, we're defined by our good deeds. Let's stay focused on that," I whispered, handing Chloe the discarded coffee cup.

"We need to find out what was in this cup. If it once contained poison, it certainly would hold traces of it."

"Right," she said, running her finger over the open book.

"We'll need three candles. The red beeswax ones. Let's see what else. One of those variety packs of bottled snake oils. Uh...three of the rainbow crystals. A piece of Egyptian parchment and three ounces of iron filings."

Jade and I quickly gathered the necessary supplies.

With Angel keenly observing, Chloe traced a triangle on the worktable with white chalk. In the center, she placed the parchment and heaped the iron filings on top.

Jade shredded the cup and placed it in a mixing bowl and stirred in the oils. Jade, Chloe, and I positioned ourselves at the points of the triangle, holding a lit candle in our left hand and a rainbow crystal in our right.

"Ready for the tongue twister?" Chloe asked. "Then repeat three times after me. In nomine of Thoth idcirco praecipio tibi ut revelet Deus absconsa tua."

Chanting the phrase three times, the candles flickered, and the crystals grew warm in our hands. The iron filings swirled in a miniature cyclone. When the particles settled back onto the parchment, they were arranged to form words. The ingredients of the cup were revealed. "Coffee, cream, sugar, caramel, digitalis."

"Bingo! We have a winner!" Jade shouted.

"That was soooo witchcraft!" Angel scolded. "Angelic remedies, my ass. I know Latin, and I know that was a spell you chanted. You even invoked Thoth, the Egyptian God of Sorcery."

"Is not! It's just a tongue-twister. Our books are filled with them," Chloe sniped back.

"Tongue-twisters? Hah! Believe what you want. All I'm saying is I don't want any of you ever holding your angelic noses up in the air when it comes to the kind of witchcraft me and my mom practice. Because it's obviously the same."

Chloe and Jade shot me nervous glances. I didn't have an answer. Could Angel be right? Had we been naively dabbling in something much darker than what we believed?

"It doesn't matter. Ours are good deeds that help others. That's what matters."

"That's right," Zane said. "Who cares if it's witchcraft or angelcraft, or whatever you call it. You are trying to save people and solve a murder."

I hid my trembling hands below the tabletop, because it certainly mattered to us. It mattered to me. But for the moment, we needed to seize on our newfound clue.

"Right. Who cares? This cup came from Kathy's, and it was used to deliver a deadly poison to Mike Schmitz. Kathy just made first place on our list of suspects."

"Hey guys," Buddy said, staring at the aftermath of our remedy. "I'm no detective, but I'm pretty sure you destroyed whatever evidence you had. I don't think you can use a bowl full of snake oil mush in court."

"Well then, it's a good thing we're not cops," Zane growled.

I had already learned how Zane's eyes could glow, telegraphing his passion. But at that moment, when I looked at him, I was suddenly alarmed.

Maybe I was even a little frightened.

Because for the first time, I witnessed a blood-red fire flash in his eyes. And something else happened—something completely unexpected. The tips of his horns poked through his thick, dark hair.

"For crying out loud, Zane. Mind your horns," Angel said.

Turning to me, she whispered, "I should've warned you. Demon's horns also pop out when they get emotional."

CHAPTER SIXTEEN

I never in a million years would've thought Kathy, the sweet, soft-spoken cafe owner, would be on the list of murder suspects.

"We have to be honest, you guys. Just because he drank a poison from a cup he bought from Kathy's café, it doesn't make her the murderer. It's circumstantial at best."

"Um, you are forgetting that she was one of Mike's black-mail victims. And she wasn't exactly surprised to learn that he croaked. You said it yourself," Chloe replied.

Angel thoughtfully twirled her wand. "I think the next question is how to confront her."

"Go for the throat!" Chloe cheered.

Zane nodded his approval.

"You want to straight up put her through an inquisition? I'm thinking a cautious approach might be better. We'll get more information if we don't start off with a confrontation." Angel shrugged.

"Right. We shouldn't let our emotions take control of the situation," I replied.

"Um...we always say that," Chloe said, waving her finger

around. We were about to get preached to. "But in the end, emotion is our modus operandi. It's the driving force behind everything we do. I mean, if it wasn't for love and empathy, would we not be using our abilities to help the good people of Angel Bay? And if it wasn't for joy and decadence, would we not wallow in pizza and romance novels? Or if it wasn't for sexual passion, would you not be getting your brains screwed out by a demon boyfriend? Or for me and Jade giving hand jobs to Daryl and Erik behind the boathouse?"

"Sweet God almighty," Angel said, rubbing her forehead.

Buddy straightened up. I swear his ears rotated with cat-like radar movements. "Hand jobs? Behind the boathouse?"

"At least she didn't bring up the blowjobs at the drive-in," Jade mumbled, flipping through the pages of one of our angelic remedy books.

"Hey, by the way. Next time, me and Daryl are taking the back seat. I thought I was going to need the jaws of life to get my head out from under that steering wheel. And you and Erik were back there laughing like hyenas." Chloe blushed. "But never mind that. The point is, we're emotional beings. We don't think, we do. I say we embrace it. Let's get Kathy in here and show her how upsetting all of this has been. To Zane, to Angel. Heck, to all of us."

"Time out," Zane announced. "Let's take Angel's approach first. But if she clams up, I'm sure someone here can whip up a truth serum."

"Fair enough," I said, seconding his plan. "We'll even bring along a truth serum as a backup."

"And don't forget to bring along one of her cups. She has no idea we destroyed the one which held the poison," Angel said.

It was early evening, just before Kathy closed up for the day, when we put our plan into motion. The last customer had just stepped out of the café when we pushed our way inside, locking the door behind us.

Kathy appeared in a doorway, just to the side of the bakery display. The late arrival of our large group certainly caught her off guard. "Sorry, but I just closed up."

We had agreed in advance, I would take the lead. "We're here on a different kind of business, Kathy."

"Oh?" she said, her hands trembling.

"It's about Mike Schmitz. Seems he didn't die of a heart attack after all," I said, displaying a paper coffee cup in a clear storage bag.

"Oh, uh, I haven't heard any news about him since." Her gaze zeroed in on the bag in my hand. "What are they saying happened?"

"That someone maybe didn't want him around anymore. And they took care of it," Zane said.

Kathy's back stiffened. Her voice trembled slightly but her tone was defiant. "Are you people insinuating I poisoned him?"

"Poison?" Angel asked, turning to us quite theatrically. "Did anyone mention poison? Why in the world would you say that, Kathy?"

"Well...because you are carrying around a cup from my store in a bag like it's evidence. What am I supposed to think?"

"You just so happen to be right, Kathy. He was poisoned. With digitalis, an extract of the foxglove flower. The same kind of flower you have blooming in your flowerbeds. That poison was served up to Mike Schmitz in a deadly caramel latte, which he purchased from you," I said.

"You can't prove that! If you could, you would've gone straight to that buffoon, Officer Daryl."

"Hey, you murdering barista!" Chloe slapped her hands on the counter. "Nobody calls my Daryl a baboon."

"Why come to me with these accusations?" Kathy asked, ignoring Chloe's behavior.

"We're giving you a chance to explain. We know you have something to do with this. If we turn it over to the cops, it's case closed. They are going to pin this on you. But maybe you have an explanation, maybe there are forces, paranormal forces involved which the police wouldn't believe," I said.

Angel whipped out her wand and zapped a cream filled Bismarck into oblivion. "But we have an understanding of the supernatural. And maybe you know where my parents are."

Kathy blinked. That's all. There was no screaming, no diving behind the counter, no fainting. None of the behavior one would expect after witnessing a scrumptious pastry being blasted to smithereens with magic.

Angel lowered her wand. "That didn't faze you. Not even a little bit?" she said, surprised and maybe a little disappointed.

"It means she's seen more impressive magic," Zane pointed out. "What you just did...well, that was nothing compared to things she's already seen."

"You're right. I have seen worse. You see, there have always been rumors quietly circulating around Angel Bay. Over the years, I've heard about magic, witches, and more unexplained things than I can count. But earlier this year, I learned a whole lot more than just rumors," Kathy said, exhaling loudly.

She seemed oddly relieved to confess her knowledge of the supernatural.

"Maybe we should all sit down." She motioned to the artfully arranged tables and chairs.

"Where to start." She stared at the napkin holder. It seemed like she was unable to make eye contact with any of us. I didn't know if that meant she was unable to be truthful, or simply ashamed for what she was about to tell us.

I clasped her hand in mine, offering her my trust. "I think we should start with the biggest thing first. Did you poison Mike Schmitz?"

"No! I mean, maybe. But I didn't know it was going to kill him," she blurted out. "I was only trying to knock him out."

"Knock him out? Why would you want to do that?"

Jade jumped into the conversation, excited to be living out a true-life crime drama. "Let me guess, out of the blue, you began to receive photos of yourself from an anonymous source, and they were seriously compromising. You found yourself the victim of a mysterious blackmail operation."

"No, that's not what happened at all. Mike and I...well, we've been...I mean, we were lovers."

I gasped. If I'd been wearing pearls, I would have clutched them.

"You had an affair? But you're married."

"Yes. I'm not proud of it. But yes, Mike and I snuck around for many years. The photos you found of me, I posed for them. I did it just for him."

"So, guys really like pictures like that?" Chloe asked. "I need you to take some nude pics of me for Daryl later." She elbowed Jade.

Jade shoved her away. "Not unless you agree to brainwash me into forgetting about it."

"What do you know about the magic? And the blackmail?"

"The magic I learned about when Mike adopted a strange dog. Besides its enormous size, it looked normal. Really, it was an extremely sweet dog. He told me he found the dog for sale on the internet. But as time went by, I noticed the dog had some very unique abilities. One evening, it was barking. Mike told it to go find something to do, to go away. Suddenly, it became invisible. Imagine my shock! I actually fainted."

"Well, that's definitely more impressive than my wand," Angel said.

"This was before I knew magic was real. Anyway, I confronted Mike. That's when he told me a very strange story. He had been contacted by someone who lived out of state. Someone from California, maybe? I'm not certain. He said it was a business arrangement. Anyway, the guy sent Mike a bunch of cash and told him to purchase a specific book from Midge."

Angel pointed at her. "Le Dragon Rouge?"

"That's exactly right. Apparently, it was a rare book of spells. Mike was told exactly what spell to use. And that was the spell to conjure up the dog. The dog was supposed to be wearing a charm on its neck, and that's the one thing the stranger wanted. As a reward, Mike could keep the book and use it for whatever purposes he wanted. Get rich, seek revenge, you name it. And that's when everything went wrong."

"I think it went wrong long before then, but go on," Jade said.

"Do you know why this stranger never came and purchased the book directly from Midge himself? Why he went through Mike?"

"Oh yeah. Mike said he asked, but was told it was none of his business. He was furious about not getting the charm. That's all I know. Anyway, Mike said the person was probably crazy."

"Did Mike ever start using the spells from the book?"

"I asked, and he told me he didn't. But as time went on, I noticed Mike suddenly had a lot of cash. Which was odd, considering how badly his business had been going. Then I came across a picture. And another, and another. Different women in nude, sexual poses. You know. Maybe I didn't have the right to be outraged, hurt, angry...but I was furious. We had a huge fight over it. Mike begged me not to break up with him. That's when he told me he'd been using the spell book to make money by blackmailing women in town. Like hypnotizing them into performing lude acts while he photographed them. They would never remember any of it, he said. So, he would never get caught. He also blamed the dog. Can you believe it? The dog used mind control powers and made him do it? Of all the ways he could've used magic to get rich, he becomes a magical pornographer and extortionist! What an asshole. Only a real sicko would do something like that. And then to say it was the dog's idea? That the dog was controlling his mind? Please. Mike had to be stopped."

"Then you killed him," Chloe said, very matter-of-factly.

"Yes, but it was an accident. I got the idea of using foxglove from the internet. I was chatting in one of my groups, asking about what herbal concoction would make a natural sleep aid. My goal was to knock Mike out. And while he was out of commission, I'd remove the poor dog from that sad cage, and I'd steal that stupid spell book. You know, put an end to his sick criminal behavior. We were through at that point anyway. I was disgusted with myself for ever having been with him for a minute. Anyway, someone in the group suggested that I use extract of foxglove. They assured me it would cause a deep, restful sleep and was completely harmless."

"Personally, you murdering your lover isn't my concern. Where are my parents?" Angel asked, tapping her wand in Kathy's direction.

"I—I don't know anything about that. Honestly, I don't."

"She's telling the truth," Zane sighed.

"She wouldn't confess to an affair and a murder, but not tell us if she knew where our parents were."

"Where's the dog?" I asked, hoping Dexter could still lead us to Ash and Eve.

"And where is the book?" Angel added.

"I have the book. It's in the bakery. The dog ran off, I have no idea where he went."

"We're taking the book," Angel said, marching around the counter.

"I suppose this is where you turn me in."

"That hasn't been decided," I said, glancing around at Zane and my friends. I have to say, I was reassured when they each nodded in agreement.

CHAPTER SEVENTEEN

*A*ngel scuffed her shoe over the sidewalk, kicking a few stray pebbles away. "I feel like we've done nothing but run around in a big circle."

"Don't be discouraged. We've learned a lot. Let's think about this mystery man who was behind Mike's foray into witchcraft. What are the clues to his identity?" I asked, turning the corner to our shop.

"His only goal was to conjure up Dexter," Chloe said.

"No, it was the magical necklace he thought Dexter would be wearing. That's what he was really after."

"My guess, it was a Hellion," Zane added. "It was someone who wanted to use the charm as leverage over the group. Does that sound like anyone you know, Buddy?"

"Um, nope. We're pretty content with things the way they are. Rocky is in charge, kind of. Along with Eve. If we ever need anything, they're happy to help."

"To me, it's obvious. The one behind this mess has to be the Marquis D'Phoenix. It just has to be. He has the motive and the knowledge. He must have found a way to reach out to Mike. Then he pays Mike to buy the book and uses it to conjure up Dexter. He wanted the charm so he could retake control of the Hellions, but it wasn't on the dog like he hoped. We just have to confront him, and I bet we'll find your parents."

"Does anyone know where the Marquis was exiled to? I think we're all familiar with the story, but I don't remember hearing about the location. I don't even know what realm."

"Oh, I think I've heard about it. I can't remember the name of it offhand, only that it sounded like an awful place."

"It must be bad if it sounds awful to a Hellion," I said. "But it doesn't matter. Now we have the book, and you can conjure up Dexter. Right, Angel?"

"I hope so. I'll just need some time to find the spell and go over the details. Can I use the backroom in your shop?"

"Of course. Make use of whatever supplies we have. If you need anything, let us know."

"I'll be happy to hang around and give you a hand, Angel," Buddy said, obviously hoping to spend some more time with her.

"That would be nice. Thanks."

Buddy's face lit up when he heard her answer. His eyes twinkled with the devilishly green glow I'd seen in Zane's.

Before entering the backroom, Angel looked over her shoulder. "How about we all meet back up in the shop in two hours?"

"Deal," Jade replied before wandering off with Chloe.

I could only hope amateur boudoir photography wasn't on their schedule.

Zane was unusually quiet, even for him. And it worried me.

Some people are easy to read. You just know by looking at them that there's something going on.

Zane was more complicated than most people I had met. It was easy to mistake his deep philosophical moments of quiet for any number of emotions. He had a way of always surprising me.

But at that moment, it didn't take a mind reader to know what he was thinking. The more time that went by without finding his parents, the less likely there would be a good outcome.

"I'd offer to make a delicious dinner for you to take your mind off things. But all I can do is order take-out or pop something in the microwave. I'm not much of a cook."

"Why don't we take a walk along the beach until some-place sounds good enough to stop in?" He twisted his fingers around mine, giving me a sad half smile.

Tiny waves lapped at my bare feet, and we turned to watch the bay shimmer in the waning twilight. The air was just chilly enough for me to appreciate Zane's warmth as I snuggled against him. Romantic? Of course. But as I looked at the first star twinkling into view, I wished we could find his parents, and lift the cloud hanging over us.

Now, I'm not going to say my childish wish was granted, or that a fairy godmother swooped in to fix everything, but we soon had a big break in the case.

"Why don't we grab a burger?" Zane pointed to Murphy's.

It was one of those inconspicuous little diners, wedged in between two buildings that rotated between startups like hair stylist, taekwondo studio, or nail salon. You name it. You know the ones that just can't seem to stick around for more than a single season.

But the meek and unpretentious little diner, which looked like it was placed there as if an afterthought, had thrived for three generations. Consequently, it was a landmark for the locals. And the go-to spot to eat when everyone answered, "Whatever you want."

Settling into a booth, I spotted the latest copy of News Hebdomad on the seat. Normally, the magazine wouldn't have interested me in the slightest. I'm the last person to stay up on current events. I will literally read the list of ingredients on a pack of gum before I pick up a weekly news periodical, but for whatever reason, this one caught my eye.

"Oh. My. God." I nearly shouted the words when I saw whose face stared back at me from the ketchup-splattered magazine cover.

The boney face, the pale complexion, the short, dark hair, the thin beard. He even wore the same fragile looking glasses.

"We can grab a different booth if something's wrong with this one," Zane offered.

Picking up the magazine, I handed it to Zane. "It's him. It's the Marquis D'Phoenix."

"Um. I can see why you might think so. The caption clearly says, 'Mark D. Phoenix, Silicon Valley's newest CEO is a rising star'. I'm sure the name is just a coincidence."

"No. Not just the name. It's him. I swear. Angel used some kind of magic spell to take us back to the moment your parents banished him. Trust me, I'll never forget his face."

Zane rolled up the magazine and turned for the door.

I was hot on his heels.

He carried the magazine like it was a baton in an Olympic event while we sprinted back to the shop in record time.

Just as we flung ourselves inside the door, a gargantuan slobbery-mouthed brown dog let out a single bark. The windows in the shop rattled and the curio cabinets shook. Skidding to a stop, I quickly made an abrupt U-turn and found myself wrapped up in Zane's arms.

"Easy, Dexter," he said, holding me with one arm and reaching out to the dog with the other. "There you go. Good boy."

Dexter greeted Zane with typical dog kisses. And I was left sickened by the wet, slapping sound of his giant tongue.

Getting showered with gobs of dog saliva certainly contributed to the yuck factor.

By the time Zane broke free, he looked as if he'd been bobbing for apples.

"He sure seems happy to see me."

Drying her hair with a towel, Angel stepped into the room. "He's happy to see all of us. I was able to conjure him up on the first try. Apparently, he wasn't too far from here. And before you even ask, I've already commanded Dexter to find Mom and Dad, he came back with nothing. Which is surprising since Dad is a demon and hellhounds are notorious demon hunters. It proves my suspicion, they are being held by someone powerful."

"We have a huge clue." Zane handed her the magazine. "Check out the guy on the cover."

"Holy outcasts! It's the Marquis D'Phoenix. In Silicon Valley?" she shouted.

"That's the place!" Buddy yelled. His memory jarred. "That's the place they sent him to. It sounds horrific, doesn't it? Silicon Valley. Yeesh."

Buddy, like the other Hellions, was more than happy to relish his simple way of life. They loved living out in nature, taking long motorcycle rides, skinny dipping in magical ponds, fluttering around the night sky on a full moon. They had few earthly possessions and no wealth to speak of.

But compared to the poor souls trapped in corporate cubicles, I suppose you could say they were blessed in a way. To them, Silicon Valley would be Hell, and a big-tech firm CEO versed in new-age management would be like working for Satan himself.

"This information makes it all the easier to question him. Don't you get it? He is on Earth. The Marquis is in the same realm we are. We can easily bring him here." Angel was suddenly energized.

Moving quickly with determination and a purpose, she opened the newly acquired grimoire. Lighting candles and smoldering pots of herbal mixtures, she raised her wand.

"You all might want to clear the room. There will be a slight...whirlwind."

"Um hey, Angel."

Something didn't make sense. If the Marquis was successful enough to make the cover of a major news outlet, why would he worry about his old life in Hell?

"I was thinking, if he is here on Earth anyway, why would..."

But it was too late to stop her. She chanted the ancient spell in Latin and twirled her wand.

A wind picked up, absolutely trashing our thoughtfully arranged backroom.

"Whirlwind, my ass!" Zane shouted over the racket and clamor. "More like a tornado!"

Buddy stood behind Angel, his big arms wrapping around her waist. He was acting as an anchor, holding her in place until the spell was over.

A blur of particles appeared in the cyclone. As the wind subsided, they clumped together until they formed a human shape. Once the winds disappeared, we saw a frightened, shivering little man sitting on the table. It was the Marquis D'Phoenix, in a navy blue business suit. "Wha—what's hap— happening to me?" he stammered.

When Angel transported us back to that moment in time, when I first saw the Marquis, I was underwhelmed by the timid villain. And seeing the sniveling little man on the table, it only reaffirmed that he certainly wasn't much of a boogieman.

"Don't play dumb with us," Angel growled. "The gig is up. We know all about your silly little plot to regain power."

"Regain power? What in the hell are you talking about?"

he asked, climbing down from the table and straightening his suitcoat.

"Reversing the spell, so you could end your banishment and take back the Hellions," I said.

The Marquis looked at each of us, his face was twisted with confusion.

"Oh, we know. And we know you needed to get the amulet, as well as the witch who placed the curse on you. We've got the amulet, but you have the witch. So, let me ask you, where are my parents?" Angel said, closing in on the Marquis.

"Slow down. Plots? Conspiracies? Listen, I have no idea what you are talking about. Yes, I was banished from my position in Hell by Eve the witch. That is true. But believe me when I say that it was the best thing that could have ever happened to me. My job in Hell sucked. I was forced into it because of hereditary succession. I've thrived in Silicon Valley. I'm living my dream. Why would I want to ruin it all?"

If it wasn't for the magazine, I doubt Zane would've believed him. But I was surprised to see him take a softer approach than his sister.

"Fair enough. So, you are saying you had nothing to do with the disappearance of our parents?"

"You're Eve's and Ash's kids? No. Of course not. I haven't seen either of them since I was banished. If I did, I'd thank them for getting me out of that hellhole."

Angel slumped into a chair, realizing we'd hit another dead end.

"Well, this turned out to be a real bust."

"Hold on. You said you only got the job through hereditary succession. After you were banished, who should've been next in line?" Zane asked.

"Next in line? Uh, I don't know for sure. I'm an only child, so it gets kind of murky. I suppose the one with the strongest claim would be my aunt, Minerva." The Marquis scratched his forehead.

"You know, now that I think about it...this sounds like something she would pull. Before you even ask, I have no idea where to find her. We haven't spoken in decades."

"Ah, we just assumed it was a man behind this. Kathy never said if she knew if it was a man or a woman who had contacted Mike."

"Minerva is a demon, so I should be able to conjure her up with this grimoire. If not, we can send Dexter out hunting for her," Angel said, slapping the book.

"I wasn't able to find Mom and Dad with either, but I can only hope for some luck with Minerva."

"Well, if you wouldn't mind sending me back. My artisanal crochet group is meeting up for kelchipoi."

"Um, kelchawhat?" Buddy asked.

"Oh, it's a kelp green chile poi, and it's just the chicest colon cleanser. It's eco-friendly and much milder than the Tijuana blasters that were so trendy last year. And with only half the seepage."

"Holy Christ," Angel whispered. "It does sound like he's been in a place worse than Hell. Maybe he should be thankful we're keeping him here until we get this all sorted out."

"That's right. You aren't going anywhere," Zane growled.

CHAPTER EIGHTEEN

*C*hloe and Jade had returned just in time to witness the strange arrival of the Marquis. I got them quickly up to speed on the case while Angel worked her magic to summon Minerva.

Zane and Buddy kept a close eye on the Marquis. Neither one of them trusted him, and I can't say that I blamed them. I didn't trust him either.

"Damn it," Angel huffed. "Something or someone is blocking me. The same way Mom and Dad's location is being blocked."

"Would Minerva be able to do that on her own?" Zane asked.

"I'm not sure. Minerva could have come across a cloaking spell that she was able to use. Time to sic Dexter on her. Let's hope he finds something out this time," she said, calling the big dog to her side.

"Find the aunt of the Marquis D'Phoenix. She's a demoness named Minerva."

"Roof!" Dexter replied.

His entire body shimmered like he had transformed into millions of shiny water droplets. Then in a puff, he was gone.

"Now, we wait," she said.

"How long does it take for a hellhound to track down a demoness? Especially one who doesn't want to be found?" I asked.

Angel shrugged. "I guess it all depends on whether he can pick up a trail. Otherwise, he'll come right back empty-handed—er, pawed. Just like last time."

Zane and I stepped out onto the front porch.

"I keep hoping for just one more big clue and we'll get there."

It was a rare moment of weakness for me. My hope had finally succumbed to my disappointment.

"This would be a good time for some of your sage wisdom. Any quotes from the classics for us?"

"One comes to mind. A Greek philosopher named Epictetus once said, 'Happiness and freedom begin with a clear understanding of one principle. Some things are within your control. And some things are not'. Maybe that applies to our situation."

"It seems like good advice in general. Simple and true. I like it," I said, staring into the starry night sky.

Buddy appeared on the porch. When he blew his nose into a handkerchief, he sounded like a goose's last dying gasp.

He truly startled me.

Even more surprising was his contribution to our conversation. "Yep, good ole Epictetus. You know, like many of the stoics, he believed philosophy was a way to live, not just some fuzzy brained theory. He taught us that life is filled with incidents which are beyond our control. Accept whatever happens undemonstratively and dispassionately. But that's not to say we aren't responsible for our own actions. Nope. Reflection and self-discipline. Those are the real keys to happiness," he said, stuffing the nasty handkerchief into the back pocket of his grease-stained jeans.

I stared at him, slack jawed, as if I'd just watched a bouquet of daisies sprout from the top of his head.

"Most demons, including Hellions, are schooled in the classics," Zane whispered.

"Roof! Roof!"

"Dexter's back!" I shouted, heading inside.

He was back. Unfortunately, he came alone.

"Roof!"

"Anyone else have a suggestion? I'm all out of tricks," Angel asked.

Chloe and Jade did their best to calm Dexter, but his barking was incessant. "This is the first dog I've ever met who has sweet slobber," Chloe said.

"Sweet slobber?" I asked.

"Yeah. Every time he licks my face, I taste sugar."

"Hold on," Jade said, lifting Dexter's lips. "Look, his mouth is full of white frosting and cake crumbs. He must have gone dumpster diving. Some demon bloodhound he turned out to be."

"Frosting? Cake crumbs?" A giant lightbulb flashed in my mind. "Kathy! Come on, guys. We're heading back to Kathy's Cafe."

Descending on the bakery like marauding Vikings, we spotted Kathy trying to make her escape through the back door.

"Gotcha, Kathy!" Angel said, accompanied by a loud splattering noise. She'd successfully pinned Kathy to the side of the building with a blast of magic, a spiderweb.

Zane forcefully dragged the quivering Marquis to the scene. "Do you recognize this woman?"

The Marquis was as surprised as the rest of us. "Aunt

Minerva? Wha-what? How? I didn't even know you could bake."

Dexter ripped open an old-time cellar access door and let out a loud bark.

"The spell. It's broken," Eve said, climbing the stairs. "Come on out, Ash. We're free."

"Mom! Dad!" Angel cheered, rushing alongside Zane to hug them.

"So, it was you the whole time. And to think I trusted you. I looked up to you," I said, feeling like I'd been made a fool of.

"Then you lied to our faces. You were the one who used Mike to get the book and the hellhound."

"I also told you the truth about what went down with Mike. He was just a means to an end. More or less. The fact that he didn't produce the amulet was bad enough, but I wasn't going to kill him over it. But then he turned out to be such a damn pervert. Well, that just sealed his fate. He had to die."

"Why did you kidnap Ash and Eve? I mean, even if you reversed the spell, the Marquis would've regained his position over the Hellions."

"Exactly. I also needed to make sure all the Hellions went back to Hell. They were more than likely to go back to Hell if the one person who looked after them on Earth suddenly vanished. It had to be a complete reversal of Eve's banishment curse. It's the only way my plan would have worked. After that, I simply take out my nephew and it would all be mine! But now, I'm screwed. And not even in a good way."

"What'll happen to her now?" I asked.

"Oh, what a tangled web we weave," Ash said, strutting in front of his entangled former captor. "I say a few hundred years playing tag with the minotaur in Purgatory's labyrinth should fit the bill for her penance. Dexter, take Minerva to her new home."

Within seconds, Dexter had pried Minerva loose from Angel's ad-hoc web, and they disappeared into thin air.

I was stunned. I'd never witnessed this type of spontaneous justice being dished out. It's not like I wanted to defend her, but it seemed she should at least go through the court system. You know, innocent until proven guilty and all that.

Eve picked up on my disbelief and placed her hand on my shoulder.

"Think about it, Emmy. Witches, demons, a supernatural dog from Hell, magic spells...there is no way justice could be delivered in the mortal world. Besides, she is a demon, and this is their way."

"That's right, Emmy. And cheer up. You should all be enormously proud. I never thought I'd see the day when angels, demons, and a witch would all work together to solve a murder and a kidnapping. You saved us, and for that, we are eternally grateful." Ash smiled.

EPILOGUE

*E*ve's spacious farmhouse kitchen was bustling with activity. We had spent the day preparing a feast to feed everyone, including the Hellions, after Angel's concert that evening.

"We really appreciate you letting us help make dinner, Eve. None of us know a single thing about cooking," I said.

Chloe finished pouring the lemony mixture into her pie crust. "That's for sure. I wanted to make Daryl's favorite dessert, but the internet wasn't any help at all. Imagine my surprise when I looked up videos on making tasty cream pies."

"My pleasure, girls. Cooking, baking, it's a lot like witchcraft when you think about it. That's why I told you to perfect your craft and you'll never want to order take out again."

Angel instructed Jade as she created the last layer on the lasagna. "Just so you know, Emmy. Mom taught my brother to cook. In fact, he's a better chef than me. So don't let him tell you anything different."

"I bet he's got the cream pie recipe down pat," Chloe mumbled.

"You know, I was thinking about Minerva and what she did. I can fully understand why she created such a twisted and convoluted plan to take control of the Hellions. But when it comes to murdering her lover? Can a man really make a woman crazy enough to kill him?"

"Honey," Eve said, placing her hands on my shoulders. "A woman will wax her vagina and rip her pubic hairs out for a man. You want to ask me that question again?"

"I suppose you have a point," I sighed.

Things had been quite content on the farm, as well as in Angel Bay.

Ash appeared to have moved in fulltime with Eve. Rocky resigned himself to admiring Eve from a distance and didn't cause any problems.

Angel relented and finally went on a date with Buddy, and then again and again—which turned into going steady.

Daryl, Chloe, Erik, and Jade were still having the times of their lives. Somehow, they managed to remain virgins, but it would be accurate to say those conditions had been reduced to a mere technicality.

And, of course, Zane and I were closer than ever. In fact, I felt like we were on the verge of a big step forward. After all, I was halo over heels in love with him.

With all of these happy distractions, a message from our heavenly supervisors caught us by surprise.

It was customarily short enough to be enigmatic.

CONGRATULATIONS ON VANQUISHING THE DEMONESS MINERVA. YOUR FIRST PERFORMANCE REVIEWS WILL BE IN TWO WEEKS.

As you can imagine, this caused quite a bit of stomach-churning anxiety among the three of us.

The fact that they knew about Minerva meant there was a

darn good chance they were aware of the other supernatural beings in Angel Bay. What would they say if they knew about me and Zane?

Was I about to be put to the test?

To add a dash of trepidation to the mix, Eve said something else that afternoon in the kitchen.

"I have to say, it's been great having you three here in Angel Bay. Oh, and the coven is dying to meet you."

"Th—the—co—coven?"

ABOUT THE AUTHOR

New York Times & USA Today Bestselling Author Melanie James is the author of more than four dozen books. She grew up in western Pennsylvania before heading off to Chicago, seeking new adventures. She found life in a big city fun for a while and even met the love of her life there. Melanie quickly tired of the hustle and bustle of the concrete jungle and settled down with her one true love in northeast Wisconsin.

Melanie has two kids, three step-kids, a beautiful daughter in-law, and the cutest grand babies. She also has two dogs and three cats who often make appearances in her books.

She loves to hear from her readers and fans. You can connect with her online:

http://www.authormelaniejames.com
http://www.facebook.com/AuthorMelanieJames

Sign up for her newsletter to get all the latest information about new releases and sales. You will also be registered for the monthly giveaway! You could be her next winner!
http://www.authormelaniejames.com/newsletter.html

If you enjoyed reading **Not Quite Demons**, she'd be eternally grateful if you'd let the world know!

REVIEW IT

Tell other readers why you liked the book, or any of her books, by leaving a review on Amazon, Goodreads, or your blogs. Reviews are of the utmost importance when it comes to distributors and retailers. They also help new readers make informed decisions when selecting a new book or author.

RECOMMEND IT

You can help others find this book by recommending it! It's easy. Just tell them! Seriously! Social media is a great platform to spread the word in reader groups and discussion boards. If you love the books or leave a review, feel free to let her know at melanie@authormelaniejames.com so she can thank you with a personal email. Your support means more than you'll ever know! Thank you!

PREVIEWS

Practically Angels

Coming of age in Heaven, what an exciting time! Especially since it's every young angel's dream to earn her wings by serving a tour in the Bureau of Angels. For everyone except Emmy Morrissey it seems. It turns out, she and a couple of others are not quite like the rest.

But Heaven has a plan for everyone—even misfits. After a bit of brief training, Emmy and her fellow oddballs are given a secret mission, to run a beachside gift shop in scenic little Angel Bay. And maybe act as guardian angels for the town. Easy-peasy, right?

They may even find time for their first forays into mortal romance, instead of just reading about it in steamy fiction. The hapless young angels soon find themselves up to their necks in supernatural mischief when they discover Angel Bay is ground zero for the paranormal.

Buy it Now

Almost Witches – Coming soon!

It's once again time for Angel Bay's annual Witch Fest! While swarms of cosplay fanatics and costumed tourists flood the town, a coven of real witches have also arrived. It seems they have a special interest in learning the secret nature of our young angels. But the bigger threat just might be the coven's daughters—a clique of mean girls who love drama.

How far are Emmy and her fellow angels willing to go in order to protect the people and town they've come to call home? Dark magic sure sounds tempting. What could possibly go wrong?

Buy it Now

Made in the USA
Columbia, SC
29 March 2021